DAY OF RECKONING

DAY OF RECKONING

Ray Hogan

Thorndike Press • Chivers Press
Thorndike, Maine USA   Bath, Avon, England

4/98 5/98 6/98

This Large Print edition is published by Thorndike Press, USA and by Chivers Press, England.

Published in 1995 in the U.S. by arrangement with
The Golden West Literary Agency.

Published in 1995 in the U.K. by arrangement with the
Author, c/o The Golden West Literary Agency.

U.S. Hardcover   0-7862-0406-0   (Western Series Edition)
U.K. Hardcover   0-7451-3029-1   (Chivers Large Print)

The text of this Large Print edition is unabridged.
Other aspects of the book may vary from the original edition.

Set in 16 pt. News Plantin by Rick Gundberg.

Printed in Great Britain on permanent paper.

British Library Cataloguing in Publication Data available

Library of Congress Cataloging in Publication Data

Hogan, Ray, 1908–
    Day of reckoning / Ray Hogan.
        p.   cm.
    ISBN 0-7862-0406-0 (lg. print : hc)
    1. Large type books. I. Title.
[PS3558.O3473D38 1995]
813'.54—dc20
                                                        94-44694

DAY OF RECKONING

1

The sun, rising cautiously from behind the ragged peaks of the hills to the east, found the day already warm. As its wave of golden light rolled swiftly down into the broad Palomas Valley and touched the weathered facades of Coyote Springs' store buildings and residences, it seemed to wake no living thing, but, instead, laid a stillness over the town even deeper than that imposed by night.

It was a deception. Marshal Wade Henry, standing just within the doorway of his living quarters, which adjoined his office and the jail, knew that no one in the settlement would still be sleeping at that moment, for this, at last, was the long-dreaded day — the hour of retribution when the town and six of its foremost citizens were to die.

It was his job to see that such did not come to pass; that had been the understanding with those marked for death — George Yeager, Pete Drum, Hugo Kline, the livery stable owner, Rufus Brock, Andy Taft, the deputy marshal, and rancher Jess Code — who had hired him only a bit more than two weeks ago.

They would not hide the pea from him, Yeager, proprietor of the general store as well as mayor, had said; they wanted him to know exactly what he was up against — an unknown killer bent on murdering them all, after which the town was to be put to the torch and burned.

Why?

Wade had voiced that logical question immediately following Yeager's statement of the facts as he and all those involved, except Code and the lawman, stood in the sweltering confines of the marshal's office. It was late July and the country was withering in the iron grip of a prolonged heat wave, the likes of which no man in the valley could recall. The storekeeper had mopped sweat from his glistening, haggard face, dug into a pocket for a creased, much handled letter, and passed it to Henry.

Wade had glanced first at the envelope's postmark: Dodge City, Kansas . . . November 20, 1874. Frowning, he had removed the ruled sheet of paper, read aloud the cramped words written upon it.

To George Yeager, Rufus Brock, Pete

Drum, Hugo Kline, Marshal Taft, and the rancher, Code. This is your death notice. On the day of August 15th you will die and your town will die with you. You will be killed one by one after which the town will be burned to the ground. This is in payment for the Dolan family that you murdered.

The letter bore no signature, of course, and Yeager, making a special trip to Dodge City shortly after its receipt, could learn nothing of the identity of the man who had sent it.

"What about the Dolans?" Wade Henry had asked.

"Bunch of squatters up the valley a ways," Drum had explained. "Blew in here after the war. From the south somewheres. Tried doing some farming but they was just too damned lazy and shiftless to make a go of it."

"Nothing more'n white trash," Yeager had said, taking up the explanation. "Jess Code caught them butchering one of his steers. There'd been thieving like that going on ever since they showed up. Finally caught them at it."

"And he lynched them," Henry said, completing the story when the storekeeper hesitated.

"Well, fact is, we all had a hand in it, I

9

reckon you'd say. Had a sort of a trial for the old man and the two boys. Right here in town. Hung them all three. Woman died a month or so later."

"You mean there wasn't a regular trial — one with a judge and jury? You just went ahead on your own?"

"Had to. Judge wasn't due here for three, maybe four months."

Rufus Brock wagged his head, then spat. "Better tell him the whole truth if we're aiming to saddle him with the chore. Fact is, we sort of got ramrodded into it by Code. He was foaming at the mouth to string them up, put a stop to all the rustling that'd been going on — not all of it by the Dolans, but he was bound to make an example of them. Said right out flat that if we didn't he'd switch his trading to Cooper's Crossing and tell all the rest of the ranchers to do the same."

"Their business is important to us," Yeager said. "You've got to understand that. Without it this place'd go busted, turn into a ghost town. We're too far west for the cattle drives, and the mines north of here petered out long ago. We've got to keep the ranchers trading with us."

Yeager's manner had changed then as a stiffness came over him. "Not that it ought to make a goddamn bit of difference to you.

10

We're hiring you to take on the job as marshal, look after this town — and us — and see that this lunatic doesn't carry out his threat."

"If there's anything to it in the first place," Brock had said. "They's a plenty that figures there's not."

Hugo Kline, wearing the customary dark clothing and flat-crowned hat of the Quakers, had shrugged. In his faintly German-accented voice he had said, "It is only right the man have all the facts."

Henry agreed. "Need them if you expect me to get the job done. One thing I'd like to know — why the date? Why did whoever it is pick August fifteenth?"

"Was on that day a year ago the hanging took place," Yeager had explained.

"Be like an anniversary," Brock noted with a wry grin. "Sure going to be a hell of a fine one for us if it happens!"

"You think maybe it won't, that it's just some kind of a joke?" Henry asked, remembering Brock's earlier words.

"Like to," Drum had answered for the others. "But we're scared to hope. Can't afford to, either."

"Why can't Taft, the law you've already got —"

"Andy ain't nothing but a deputy, and a part-time one at that. Regular marshal, Hayden, was out of town on the day it all took place. Taft was just filling in for him."

"Done all right, too," Drum said. "Fact is, old Andy tried to stop us. Wish'd to hell now that we'd listened to him."

"Where's Hayden?"

"Quit cold. Pulled out on us a month ago. Said he didn't want no part of it."

"Better for us he did leave," Yeager said. "All he was good for was jailing drunks on Saturday nights and keeping the drifters moving."

"Can't hardly blame him," Brock had said. "We all been sweating it out ever since that letter come and it's got worse the last few weeks. Been like a sticker that gets under a man's hide and starts festering."

"We kept it from the town for a while — two, maybe it was three months," the storekeeper went on, "but it slipped out —"

"Was old Andy," Brock had said. "Shooting off his mouth."

The mostly silent Kline had raised a cautioning hand. "Thee doesn't know that for sure now, Rufus —"

Brock, who operated the feed and seed store, swore. "Maybe you don't but I —"

"Well, whoever," Yeager had said, "it got out. Folks have been walking on eggs ever since. Even had a few pull stakes and clear out entirely. Said they couldn't afford to take a chance on losing everything they had."

"Been a damn sight more leaving than coming," Drum observed sourly. "Can count at least nine families that've moved on and only three — that real-estate fellow, Forbes; Cook, over at the Alamo Saloon; and Miss Camille — coming in."

"You're forgetting the gunsmith — Sutton."

"Can't hardly count him and his missus. They got here about the same time the letter did — a bit afterwards, maybe."

Wade Henry had given that thought. "There a chance one of them could be the killer?"

"Who the hell knows? Sure wouldn't be Miss Camille. She's an old maid that moved in and opened up a ladies' dress shop. And it'd hardly be Burl Sutton and his wife. Like I said, they've been living here since around the first of the year."

"What about Forbes and Cook?"

Yeager shrugged. "Known Cook for a long time — from over in Texas. And Forbes, well, he just ain't the type."

"Type — hell!" Brock had exploded. "What's that mean? There some way you can spot a man walking around with murder on his mind? He blowed in here less'n a month ago, and for my money, he'll bear watching."

"Maybe, but it's pretty hard to connect him up with the Dolans. Eastern fellow. Can't see him being any relation to them trashy squatters."

Pete Drum, who ran the hotel, had then said, "My guess is that the looney, whoever he is, ain't got here yet. He'll show up right on the day — the fifteenth — like he said in the letter. Be the way he'll work."

George Yeager had sighed, taken the letter from Henry's hands, folded it, and thrust it back into his pocket. "Well, whatever, we got us a hell of a problem and we're looking for a good man to take care of it. What do you think, Henry?"

"We've give you the facts," Drum had added. "And you know what we expect. We make it through, you've got the marshal's star permanent. If we don't there won't be no town, and no job."

Wade Henry had taken the job. At twenty-eight years old he was still footloose, a drifter, a failure at everything he had undertaken. Now there was an awareness upon him born of a searching moment when he had traveled the dim corridors of his mind, lonely as the wind, and assessed the past and calculated his future; the day had come when he must settle down. He must anchor himself and make good

— or look forward to a life of long, dusty trails, of friendless, hostile towns, and emptiness.

Such called for a job, one he must hold and be a success at; only by so doing could he carve for himself a niche in the scheme of life. As luck would have it, this one chance, possibly a final chance, presented a near impossible task, but he did not question it. He was only grateful for the opportunity to end the years of aimless wandering and still the nagging dread that had come to occupy his being and plague his thoughts.

He had said yes, and they had sworn him in, pinning the star of authority upon his breast. Now, as he stood there in the doorway of his quarters, a forefinger absently tracing the smooth track that a scarring bullet had burned across his cheek, a deep sigh slipped from his lips.

The time of waiting was over. The day that Coyote Springs feared, and with it the hours during which he would face his own personal moment of truth, were at hand. The future for both would stand or fall in accordance with the outcome.

2

7:00 A.M.

Wade Henry stepped from the doorway of his quarters into the silent, heat-punished street, glanced at the large clock that George Yeager, in an act of civic beneficence or perhaps as a form of subtle advertising, had mounted in the window fronting his store. Even at that early hour tension filled the town, and fully aware of it, Wade's mouth drew into a grim line. It would be a long day.

Harsh sunlight glinted off the star he wore. Pausing, he took a moment to remove it and fasten it inside his shirt pocket. He would be patrolling the settlement on watch for an unknown killer; there was no wisdom in giving even the smallest advantage to the faceless intruder.

Moving on, a tall, lean man with rough-cut features and dark eyes that relentlessly probed all that lay before him, he drew abreast the jail and again halted. Reaching for the knob, he flung back the door, permitting the heated,

16

stagnant air trapped within during the night to escape. The building was of frame, supporting a corrugated metal roof; in the hours to come it would be near unbearable inside and there was no point in making it worse by leaving the place closed.

Continuing slowly, he mounted the steps to the porch of the structure next in line, Pete Drum's Enterprise Hotel, which offered the best restaurant facilities as well as boasting the largest saloon and gambling casino in Coyote Springs. Entering, he made his way to that portion relegated to the café.

Picking a course through the scattering of tables with their red-checked cloths and hardback chairs, Henry crossed the deserted room to his customary position at the window and sat down. Mrs. Wingate, the portly waitress, appeared at once, took his order for steak, eggs, and coffee in her usual too-early-in-the-morning-to-be-friendly attitude, and retired grumpily to the kitchen.

A moment later Drum, in the cook's department for some reason, came through the connecting doorway and walked briskly to where Henry sat. He brought with him a small pot of coffee, and nodding to the lawman, filled the two cups on the table and settled onto a chair.

The hotelman, his hand shaking noticeably

as he raised the coffee to his lips, managed a strained smile.

"Reckon this here's the day we've all been waiting for."

Wade inclined his head slightly. "By sundown we'll know if that letter was a joke or not, I expect."

"It's no joke," Drum said, staring off into the street. "That sonofabitch, whoever he is, means it. . . . You see Jess Code yesterday?"

"Rode out to his place," the lawman replied. "Told him I figured it'd be smart for him to stay inside his house today. He same as told me to go to hell. Said nobody was making him crawl into a hole."

Drum ran splayed fingers through his thinning red hair. He was a spare man with a veined face and blue eyes that were almost colorless.

"Sounds like him — too damned big to be scared by anything, or anybody. Marshal, I don't mind admitting to you that I am — and plenty. Having that goddamn letter hanging over my head all this time has sure got to me."

"Can see how it would," Henry said, taking a swallow of his coffee.

"You got any special plans for how you aim to handle things today?"

"Wait and watch, about all I can do. Talked

to all the others same as I did you and Code, told them it'd be best to stay out of sight. Figure that'll force the killer to do the moving around and give me a chance to spot him. I'm open to suggestions."

Drum wagged his head. "Seems you're doing about all a man could do."

"Aim to be walking the town, making the rounds all day, starting soon's I get my breakfast eat."

"Reckon you'll have some help there. Everybody's on the lookout for strangers. Any show up you'll hear about it fast."

"What I'm hoping for, but I'm not figuring too strong on it. Take a look at that street. Nobody in sight. By this time there's usually folks moving about. They're scared, same as if they'd been named in that letter, and are staying under cover."

"I know," the hotelman murmured. "Guess you can't blame them."

"I'm not — just saying they figure it's my job, and I'm looking at it the same way."

Mrs. Wingate reappeared, frowning as she brought the plate of food, plumping it down irritably on the table before Henry. "Biscuits ain't ready," she announced. "Light bread'll have to do."

"It'll do," Wade replied, and smiling, watched the woman move away.

"I'm asking you to just overlook Maude," Drum said, apologizing as he got to his feet. "Would run her off the place, the way she treats my customers, only I ain't got the heart. Widow woman. Got a couple of kids to raise."

"Never bothers me," Henry said, beginning to eat his meal.

"Glad you feel that way. . . . Well, Marshal, good luck."

"Same to you," the lawman said without looking up. "Just mind what I've told you and leave the rest to me."

Pete Drum cut back through the doorway that led into the hotel lobby and disappeared. Henry ate slowly, steadily, refilling his coffee cup twice during the process, and when finished, he rose and left the café. His check would be added to those already accumulating for the month, settlement of which would be made on the first, when he received his pay.

He returned to the porch of the Enterprise, swept the street with a swift glance, and stepped down into the loose dust. Keeping to the edge of the board sidewalk, he moved on, passing in front of Gibson's Hardware Store, the Gem Bakery, and a butcher shop run by a man named Mondragon. He could see shadowy figures in the depths of each, but none appeared to note his presence.

Following the meat market was a narrow

passageway that separated the Enterprise and the lesser adjoining structures from the two-story building housing Sutton's Gun Shop. Scanning the length of the passageway and finding it empty, he continued his slow march along the eerily hushed street.

As he drew abreast Sutton's the screen door opened abruptly and Willa Sutton, almost as if she had been waiting for him, walked out onto the roofed gallery. She had a square of cloth in her hands, went through the motion of shaking it, and then, turning, saw him.

"Oh — Marshal!" she said, smiling. "You startled me."

The sunlight on her auburn hair shone brightly, changed it to a rich gold, and her eyes — a clear, gray-blue — seemed lighter against her dusky skin.

"Just starting my rounds," he said.

She sobered at once. "It's the day, isn't it?"

"The day," he replied.

Henry had thought much about Willa Sutton during his short residence in Coyote Springs. That hers was not a happy marriage had become quickly apparent; that she was also attracted to him as he was to her was also evident; and more than once he had wished she'd come into his life before meeting and marrying the man who was her husband.

21

But it hadn't been that way, and she was another man's wife and therefore beyond his reach — if not his thoughts.

"I've some fresh coffee on the stove," she said, moving back to the door. "Burl's just finishing his. Won't you come in for a cup?"

He'd had plenty but it wasn't in him to refuse her. Mounting to the gallery, Henry followed her through the small, front shop with its glass display case of pistols and knives, and wall racks and shelves of long guns and boxed ammunition, to the rooms beyond where living quarters were maintained.

Sutton, a thick-shouldered man with dark hair and strangely contrasting light eyes, glanced up from the table where he was thumbing through a catalog. He nodded, then grinned.

"Morning, Marshal. Guess this is going to be your busy day."

Wade settled himself on a chair, trying not to be conscious of Willa moving about, getting a cup, placing it before him, and filling it from a small, white enamel pot.

"I'm looking for the worst," he said. "That way I won't be surprised."

Sutton laid aside the dog-eared book. "You really figure this killer will come, do what he promised?"

"Far as I'm concerned, he will. Lives of six

men involved — and one of them's actually innocent."

Sutton's thick brows lifted. "Who's that?"

"Taft, the deputy. He was here when those lynchings took place — regular marshal was out of town. He tried to stop it."

Burl Sutton nodded, sipped at his coffee. "Hadn't heard about that. About the lynchings, sure, but the details they seem to keep sort of quiet. Can't say as I blame Yeager and the others. Bad thing to happen."

Wade touched Willa, now seated across the table, with his glance. "Good coffee," he murmured, and then: "Reckon something like this could never happen in St. Louis."

She shuddered. "It's horrible — terrible! I never dreamed anything like this could go on."

"This is the frontier, Willa," Burl said dryly. "We never saw anything like this back there because it had all passed on. The town had become civilized. But there was a time when it would've been ordinary."

Henry took another swallow of his coffee. "How long were you in business there?"

"Couple of years —"

"It was my home," Willa said. "Burl and I met there, were married. That was two years ago, too. Have you ever been to St. Louis?"

"Once — passing through. No chance to look it over."

"It's a fine place. Beautiful in the summer as well as in the winter. Lots of trees and flowers, and grass everywhere. You liked it, didn't you, Burl?"

Sutton nodded absently. "Good place to live but not to do business. Reason I moved out here. . . . How do you plan to cope with this — this danger, Marshal?"

Wade finished the last of his coffee, held up a hand to stay Willa as she reached for the pot.

"Just keep my eyes open and walk the street and alleys. Sooner or later I ought to turn up the killer."

"As good a plan as any," Sutton said approvingly. "See you're wearing your badge out of sight. Smart. No sense inviting a bullet — and a lawman would be somebody he'd like to get out of the way first off so's he'd have no interference."

Wade smiled. "That's how I see it. I'm no braver than the next man, and I don't need to wear a star for the folks here in town to show I'm the law."

"You'll still be taking a terrible chance," Willa said, toying with a spoon. "Isn't there some other way?"

"Expect the marshal knows his job," Burl

cut in. "Best we leave things like that to him."

"Of course, but —"

"I'm no hand to take chances," Henry said smiling again as he came to his feet. "Found out a long time ago that getting shot at wasn't the most comfortable feeling a man could have."

Sutton rose also. "This your first go at being a lawman?"

"Town marshal, yes. Was a deputy sheriff for a spell once. Tried my hand at a few other chores, too — riding shotgun for a stage line, bullion wagon guard, things like that. Fact is, I expect I've done a little of everything."

"And become master of none," Sutton commented pointedly.

Wade Henry saw the flush mount quickly in Willa's cheeks. He shrugged. "That's how it goes. Some men find what they want early in life, others don't."

"Found my place at twelve," Sutton said briskly. "Ran off to sea — British merchantman. Knocked around for a few years, then wound up in Germany. Learned my gunsmithing there. Been following the trade ever since."

"Lucky man," Henry murmured, moving toward the door. "Can think of a few I know who're still looking and will probably keep on until they're dead."

"What about you?" Willa asked, watching Burl cross to the stairway rising against the back wall of the room and leading to his workshop on the upper floor. "Is being the marshal here what you're looking for?"

Henry paused, hand on the dust-grayed screen door. "I'll settle for it," he said, moving on. "Obliged for the coffee."

3

He was more than willing to settle for the job as Coyote Springs' lawman, Wade Henry thought as he stepped into the open. Willa had no idea of just how important it was that he make good this time, and have the right to claim permanently the star pinned inside his pocket.

Halting in the driving sunlight, he probed the still silent, deserted street with his gaze. Townspeople were up and about, he knew, but they were being careful to stay out of sight, either remaining in their homes or inside their businesses where they had living quarters. There had been those who scoffed at the idea of a killer slipping into the settlement and exacting the penalty he had pledged, but now that the time was at hand they were as noticeably scarce as were those who had been frank to admit their fear.

Wade grinned bleakly at the thought, swung his glance to the building adjacent to Sutton's — Miss Camille . . . Ladies Ready to Wear

. . . Hats and Dresses. The shades were still drawn over the windows, and she had not as yet opened for business, if indeed, she planned to do so that day. He walked on at a slow pace, eyes reaching beyond the vacant lot that lay immediately ahead, to Hugo Kline's livery stable, to the corrals in the rear where a half a dozen horses stood slack-hipped in the rising heat, to the empty wagonyard along its side.

Kline, moon-face sober, met him as he turned into the runway that extended the full length of the sprawling barn.

"A good day to thee, Marshal," he rumbled in his thick voice. He made a motion toward the small office built in the corner of the structure overlooking the street. "Coffee is ready."

Wade shook his head, followed the heavy-set stableman into his cobwebby, cluttered business quarters.

"Appreciate the offer but I've had about all I can carry for a bit."

Kline nodded, poured himself a mug full from a pot simmering on the plate of a small, cast-iron stove. The room was already sweltering hot and the fire was steadily making it worse.

The stableman brushed at the sweat on his face, took a swallow of the black liquid. "There is something?"

"No, just making the rounds," Henry said,

28

dropping back to the doorway and looking into the murky depths of the building. It was considerably cooler there in the opening. "Aim to come by pretty often today but I want to tell you again it'll be smart for you to stay inside your place."

"That I will do," Kline said.

"Asking you to keep your eye out for strangers coming into town, too. Get word to me if you spot somebody you don't know."

"Yes —"

"Don't come yourself. Send your stable boy or the hostler. Probably find me somewhere along the street, or at the jail."

The old Quaker stared thoughtfully into his mug of coffee and nodded. "Do thee do this alone?"

"My job."

"Is it not also the job of the deputy?"

"Taft? Maybe, but I've told him to stay in his shack. He's on that list, remember, and letting him walk the street would make it easy for the killer to scratch off the first name."

Hugo Kline's massive shoulders stirred. "I fear he will not heed thee, Marshal. It is a duty he feels."

"Duty or not, he's staying under cover. Don't want to be worrying about him. . . . Expect I'd best have a look through the barn while I'm here."

The stableman set his cup aside. "It is kind of you, Marshal," he said in his solemn way.

Henry made his tour of the structure, going through the dark corners of the ground floor as well as the loft, but found nothing. He paused long enough to talk with the hostler, who was in the rear cleaning a stall, and passed on a warning to him. The man listened woodenly and made no reply. It was evident from his manner that if an emergency arose his sole interest would be his own well being.

Wade circled the building once, crossed the narrow passageway on its north wall, and slanted toward the vacant structure, once occupied by a print shop, that lay next in line on that side of the street.

Trying the front door he found it barred. He drew up sharply. Earlier that day it had been open when he checked. Immediately a stream of caution began to flow through him. Resisting the urge to hurry, he moved on leisurely until he reached the corner of the building. Rounding it quickly, he made his way to the rear door. Halting, he drew his pistol, and gripping the cracked knob in the thin panel, he threw it open and stepped inside.

A horse standing against the wall to his left shied at his abrupt appearance. A few steps farther along a man sprang upright.

"Keep your hands where I can see them,"

Henry snapped.

The man sighed deeply. "Sure, Marshal."

"Now, move out here into the light."

"Sure —"

Wade watched the man amble into the shaft of sunlight flooding in through the open doorway. He was well up in years — thin, iron-gray hair, slack, lined face, and sunken, watery eyes. His clothing was worn, crudely patched in places, and the heels were almost gone from his run-down boots. He wore no gun.

"What're you doing here?"

The man shrugged. "Grabbing a night's sleep. Plumb tired of roosting in the brush."

"Where you headed?"

"No place — anyplace."

A drifter. . . . A bitter thought passed through Wade Henry's mind: *This could be me fifteen, twenty years from now.* Turning his head he glanced at the battered saddle dropped near the horse. The boot was empty of its rifle and there was no gun belt.

"Where's your iron?"

"Sold the rifle back up in Raton. Ain't had me no six-gun for quite a spell. Sold it in Kansas somewhere. Man's got to eat."

"Broke?"

"Flat-assed busted, Marshal. Was hoping maybe I'd find me a job around here.'

"No chance," Henry said, holstering his

weapon. "You picked the wrong time to show up in this town. Got a name?"

"Kincaid. Folks generally call me Texas Jack. You jugging me?"

Henry dug into his pocket, brought forth a silver dollar. "No, but I want you gone." He flipped the coin to Kincaid. "Restaurant's across the street. Get over there and have yourself a meal — then move out. Understand?"

Texas Jack fondled the silver dollar between a thumb and forefinger, and nodded hastily. "Yes sir, Marshal, I'll be doing just like you say — eating myself a bite and riding on. Sure am obliged to you."

"You've got one hour," Henry said gruffly and turned to the door, still disturbed by the thought that in Kincaid he could be seeing himself in the future should failure again attend his efforts in Coyote Springs.

He crossed quickly to the next building, a narrow rock and wood affair housing a bootmaker named Zakowski. He found the man at his last working on footwear for one of the ranchers, and after repeating his request to be on the alert for strangers, Wade continued on to the last structure on that side of the street, a dilapidated, rag-tag saloon run by a Tennesseean known, unaccountably, as Arky.

The old man was in his living quarters in

the rear of the saloon, alone and having himself a breakfast that appeared to consist mostly of fried potatoes.

"Set, fill your plate," he invited as Henry entered the room.

The lawman expressed his thanks and shook his head. "Just finished."

"Got a plenty," Arky said, sleeving away the sweat on his face. He studied Henry briefly, sucking noisily at a tooth. "Reckon you're out looking for this here killer folks is expecting."

"That, and asking you to keep your eye out for a stranger coming in," Wade replied. "You being the last place on this side of the street it's likely you'll be the first to spot him."

"If'n there is somebody coming —"

The lawman shrugged. He had forgotten that Arky was one of the skeptics who took no stock in the belief that vengeance was to be visited upon the settlement.

"Like to figure on that but it's too big a risk."

"Naw, you're wrong there," the saloonman said confidently. "Ain't nobody that crazy. Who'd it be? Knew them Dolans some myself. Old Jeb used to come in here for his liquor. When they strung him and his boys up, and the old woman died, there weren't nobody left. Was the end of the Dolan family."

"Could have had relatives somewhere — a

33

brother maybe, or another son."

"Ain't likely. Old Jeb would've mentioned it."

"He talk much when he was drinking?"

Arky leaned back in his chair, again wiping at his face. "Well, can't say as he was the talking kind, but I'm plenty sure he'd a said something about it if he'd had other kin. Way I see it, it's just some yahoo having hisself a big laugh."

Wade Henry smiled. "Suit me fine if it turns out that way. Just the same, I'm asking you to watch for strangers, get word to me if any show up. I figure your saloon'll be the first place a man would stop if he rode in from the north."

Arky rose to his feet, a large, bulky man in clothing badly in need of cleaning. "Be right pleased to do that, Marshal, but like I said, everybody's all riled up over nothing far as I can see. There ain't nothing going to happen."

"Hope you're right," Henry said, and stepped out into the sunlight.

4

The lawman halted at the corner of the saloon, and tilting his hat forward to shade his eyes, spent a long minute exploring the dusty void baking in the hot sunlight between the two rows of buildings. Tension, seemingly keeping pace with the steadily climbing heat, was now almost tangible in its intensity.

Shrugging off the tautness that was stealthily creeping through him, he brought his attention around to the structure directly across from Arky's, the final store on the opposite side. The faded sign mounted on its front read *Gents' Clothing*. It was run by a man named Simon, a squat, balding individual who had originally been a pack-peddler but had finally been able to quit the trails and settle down.

Henry moved to the doorway, entered, and paused just inside. Simon emerged from the back, his lined features expressionless.

"There something you want, Marshal?" he asked, stationing himself behind a counter

35

upon which were stacks of denim work clothing.

"Dropped by to see if everything was all right," Wade said, removing his hat and mopping at its leather band.

"There is no trouble here —"

"Not exactly what I meant. Like to know if you've seen anybody new around — strangers."

"In the café — there is a man —"

"Know about him. Any others?"

"No. . . . There will be trouble, you think?"

"Got to figure there'll be — play it safe."

The older man sighed deeply. "It is bad. For many years I dream of a store like now I have. It is hard to think of fire — of losing it."

"Be doing my best to keep that from happening."

"I know, but it is a hard job to protect a town. And you are one man only."

"Far as I know, only one man wrote that letter. Makes it even, but you can help by letting me know quick if you see any strangers."

Simon bobbed. "All right, Marshal. I will send somebody — it is best I stay in my place — fire is a bad thing."

"Just let me know," Henry said, and stepped back out onto the sidewalk.

Adjoining the store, in the same low-roofed building, was the Star Café. Wade could see the drifter Kincaid eating his meal at the counter. Stopping long enough to speak with the proprietor, Orrin Gray, and repeating his request to watch for any newcomer, he moved on to the third set of business quarters in the structure.

Wayland, the town's only physician, occupied the front quarter of the building, and the sign on his office door advised that he was away on a call and would return by noon.

Emory Schmitt maintained his undertaking parlor in the remaining portion of the area, and Wade found him engaged in constructing a coffin in preparation for any eventuality. Three more of the narrow, pine boxes were stacked in the corner of his workshop.

He would keep a sharp lookout, Schmitt promised, and call upon him if needed. Wade moved on after a brief conversation with the solemn-faced man, relieved to get away from the gloomy establishment.

Hesitating in the vacant lot separating that cluster of buildings from its neighbor to the south, Cook's Alamo Saloon, the lawman again allowed his glance to run the street — still silent, still deserted, its life completely inhibited by the threat that hung over it.

There were people along its length, but they

were little more than shadowy movements behind windows, and occasionally he caught a glimpse of white, strained faces peering out at him.

Fear had seized the town, was holding it in a viselike grip, but he knew it was useless for him to try to reassure all those who had fallen victim to it. They were aware of the killer's promise — and he was, himself, a stranger to them, unknown and untried. That they placed little faith in him and his abilities was to be expected, for how could they be sure he had it in him to rise to the challenge and stand between them and the danger all were anticipating? They could only wait and hope — the same as he was, Wade thought grimly.

He crossed to the Alamo. The front door of the saloon was locked and he made his way to the rear. He found Cook sitting in a chair under one of the many cottonwood trees that dotted the valley, smoking his pipe.

The Texan was one of the three who had arrived in Coyote Springs within the last ninety days, and although George Yeager had vouched for him, Henry was accepting the storekeeper's endorsement with some reservations.

With the exception of Miss Camille, he felt he could not afford to close the door on any possibility, and that he must view with suspicion all newcomers to the settlement. The killer could be clever enough to move in well ahead of the specified day and thus avoid being obvious.

Cook greeted him with a drawling "Good morning," and jerked a stubby thumb at a nearby bench. "Have a seat. You reckon this heat's ever going to break?"

Wade shook his head. Leaning against the tree, he made known the reason for his visit. When he had finished the saloonman nodded.

"Why sure, you can depend on me, Marshal. You got my help — every last pound of it. Wish't I'd had time to send for some friends of mine in San Antone. They'd knowed how to handle a sidewinder like this here jasper that wrote that letter."

Henry shrugged. "Any idea what they'd do?" he asked in a dry voice.

Cook looked startled, hawked, and spat into the dust. "Well, no, can't say as I do. Prob'ly just keep their eyes peeled."

"Just what I'm doing," the lawman said, and smiling, moved on to the building next in line, the one occupied by Carson Forbes.

As he was already at the rear of the structures, Wade knocked first at the door there. When no response came, he circled to the front where the land broker had established

39

his office. That door, too, was locked. Looking through the dust-filmed window, he could see the man was not inside.

Turning about, Wade stared thoughtfully off across the flat beyond the creek to the west of the town. Forbes was the third of the recent arrivals, and from the start there had been a stir of doubt in his mind concerning the man, although it was difficult to see how he would have any connection with the squatter family.

Forbes professed to be a land developer, claimed he was interested in buying up property for eastern investors. Coyote Springs had a great future, he was sure, and hinted that it would one day soon have the benefit of a railroad. Such would turn the settlement into a thriving city.

No one else had heard of the possibility, and it was received with a mixture of skepticism and hope. Forbes did appear to know whereof he spoke, and presented a convincing front. He was well dressed at all times, seemed to possess money, as well as indicating there was plenty more available should he have need of it.

He had bought up nothing in the way of farms and ranches so far, but of course he had been in town for only a short while — a month, more or less — and it was only reasonable to think he had as yet found nothing to his liking insofar as investments were concerned.

It was likely that was where he was at that moment — off somewhere in the valley having a look at available property before the heat made riding uncomfortable. He must have made an early start, however, Wade decided; he himself had been up and about long before sunrise and had seen no riders leave town.

The lawman wheeled sharply, hearing the soft thud of a horse's hooves in the deep dust of the street. As he came about, his hand dropped to the pistol on his hip. It slid away, a tight smile pulling at his lips. It was only Kincaid, the drifter, moving on. His meal over, he was leaving as ordered.

Kincaid raised a hand, touching a forefinger to the ragged brim of his stained hat.

"*Adios,* Marshal," he murmured as he drew abreast. "Obliged to you — and luck."

Feeling the quick, leaping tension that had surged through him fade, Wade Henry nodded. "So long," he replied.

5

Luck, Henry thought wryly, was something he'd be needing in wagon-load quantities — luck in being aware of the killer's arrival, luck in getting him located, and luck in stopping him before he could carry out his plans.

Walking on slowly in the tense, heat-laden hush, he crossed the passageway between the building occupied by Carson Forbes and its neighbor, Yeager's General Store.

He could see the merchant inside — portly, gray mustache, gray spade beard, graying curly hair. Everything about George Yeager bespoke prosperity and authority. There was little wonder that he was the acknowledged leader and mayor of the community. Little wonder, too, Wade decided, that he had been in the forefront with rancher Jess Code in the Dolan lynchings; his destiny lay in the continued success of Coyote Springs — or its failure.

"Anything on him yet?"

The storekeeper's hard, direct voice hit

Wade head on as he pulled back the screen door and stepped into the darker, somewhat cooler interior of the building. The place was well stocked, with shelves and counters piled high with merchandise. Someone had once remarked that all the other stores in the settlement could close down and the people of the Palomas Valley would still be able to fill their needs at Yeager's.

"Nothing," Henry said, mopping at his face and neck with a bandana. Of all the men he had met in Coyote Springs he felt the least cordiality toward the autocratic merchant.

"Seems you ought to by now." Yeager paused, glancing over his shoulder at the elderly man, ordinarily referred to as Old Amos, busy at that moment stacking canned goods on a shelf. "Who was that saddletramp that was riding down the street?"

"Drifter. Spent the night in the print shop building. Told him to move on."

"You sure he ain't got nothing to do with it?"

"Reckon I am," Wade drawled.

"Ought to keep an eye on him just the same, be damned sure he keeps going. Anybody else come in during the night?"

"Haven't turned up anybody —"

"Well, if that saddlebum rode in without you spotting him, others could, too!"

"Maybe, but wasn't my plan to walk the street all night."

Yeager folded his arms across his chest. "Maybe you should have. That's what we're paying you for."

Wade Henry's jaw tightened. "You'll get your money's worth."

"Ain't what I'm interested in!" the merchant snapped. "Staying alive, that's what's counting with me."

"Counts with me, too — keeping all of you alive. I can do it if you'll all listen to me, do what I tell you, and stay out of sight."

"How the hell is a man going to do that and take care of his business? He's got to eat, and now and then make a trip to the outhouse, don't he?"

Wade shrugged. "Make other arrangements. Point is you've got to hide, keep from showing yourself. Not hard for you to do — just keep away from the front of your store and that window — let Old Amos wait on trade."

"Trade!" Yeager echoed. "There plain ain't none! Started falling off yesterday, and there ain't been a soul in here this morning. That goddam Jess Code — wish't now I'd never —"

"Too late to be stewing over that. You see Forbes today?"

The storekeeper frowned. "Nope. Not since

yesterday. Ain't he in his office?"

"Place is locked tight, front and back."

Yeager gave that consideration, then shook his head. "Probably out looking over some land."

"Likely."

"How about Kline and the others?"

"Talked to everybody but Brock so far this morning. Giving them the same advice and warning that I gave you — to stay under cover. Only way we can draw the killer into the open, force him to show his hand so's I can move in on him."

"Suppose so," Yeager said peevishly. "Hell of a note when a man can't look after his own business, however. You just be damn sure you're on your toes."

"Expect to be," Wade replied, anger stirring through him once again as he took his leave.

The structure where Bill Dollarhide operated his barbershop stood next in the line, and Henry paused there, peering through the screen at the slight, narrow-faced man engaged in giving himself a shave.

"Asking you to keep your eyes peeled — same as I did yesterday," he called through the dust-clogged mesh.

The barber came half around, soapy lather clothing his cheeks and chin with a snowy

45

beard, his razor poised.

"Just what I'll do, Marshal. . . . You're next if you're planning to part with them whiskers."

"They'll have to wait," Henry answered, and walked on to Brock's Feed Store in the adjoining building.

He entered the open doorway. Brock was in the small office that was halfway back in the narrow structure. The back door had been propped open, and a faint, cool draft was pushing through making the interior a bit more pleasant.

"Rufe," he said, halting.

"Right here —"

Brock's voice sounded thick, muffled. Wade circled around to face the feed store man. He was holding a half-empty quart bottle of whiskey, and from his disorderly appearance and the slackness in his features it was evident he had been drinking throughout the night.

"They's something you're wanting, Marshal?" he asked haltingly.

"Just making the rounds, seeing that everybody's all set."

"I'm fine, Marshal, fine."

Henry stepped closer, took the bottle from Brock's hand, and placed it on the rolltop desk standing against the wall.

"Not going to help much, swigging that

stuff," he said, surprised and puzzled by the man's behavior. It was clear he had lost his nerve.

"Best way I know of for a fellow to get his mind off'n his troubles."

"And a good way to get himself killed. Need you in good shape today."

"I'll be all right," Brock said doggedly, taking up the bottle again. "Aim to do just what you told me, crawl in this here hole and pull it in after me. I'm — I'm depending on you not letting nobody come in to get me. Ain't that what you're figuring to do?"

Wade nodded. "Be watching over all of you. Could be for nothing — which is what I'm hoping."

Brock stared at the bottle clutched so tightly in his hand that the knuckles showed white. "There's somebody coming for us, Marshal. Know that. Got a feeling about it, and them feelings ain't never wrong."

"Always a first time," Henry said, dropping a hand on the man's shoulder. He jerked his thumb at the back door.

"Expect we'd best close and lock that. Can't watch both ends of the place at the same time."

"Sure, sure," Brock said absently. "Anything you say."

Wade crossed to the rear of the building. Kicking aside the brick placed there to keep the panel open, he glanced at the lock. "No key. It around somewhere?"

Rufus Brock frowned. "Seems I recollect seeing it the other day. You sure it ain't in the lock?"

"Not here," Wade replied, dropping back to the desk.

He made a search of its surface and the drawers, but failed to turn up the missing key. Brock watched him in wooden silence until he had finished, and then wagged his head.

"It's all right, Marshal, I'll find it in a couple of minutes."

"Start looking now," Henry said in a stern voice, again taking the liquor from the man and setting it aside. "If you can't find it, push something up against the door, block it, understand?"

"Sure do. Don't you go worrying none about me."

Wade Henry studied the man for a long moment, and then wheeling, doubled back to the front entrance. He'd check again on the door later when he repeated his rounds, just to be certain Rufe had secured the door. There was no sense in making it easy for the killer, if and when he came.

Stepping out into the driving sunlight, he walked off the landing, crossed the weedy, vacant lot that separated the feed store from the last building on that side of the street. It was an old saloon, now abandoned and going to ruin under the relentless hammering of time and weather.

The roof had long ago fallen in; doors had been removed and one wall sagged inward dangerously. There was little possibility of anyone finding either shelter or a hiding place within it, but the lawman made his check of the premises, nevertheless.

Finding it empty and baking silently in the heat, Wade turned toward the jail and his office which stood directly opposite. A long sigh escaped his lips. He was satisfied the killer had not slipped into the settlement during the night; and he had repeated his warning to the men involved.

He'd go now and have a look through the residential area and the brushy groves that surrounded the town.

6

He crossed the street slowly, eyes ceaselessly probing the hushed canyon laying between the stark, seemingly deserted buildings. Like a ghost town, he thought, or one about to become such. Reaching the jail, he mounted the short landing and stepped through the doorway into its furnacelike interior. He came to an abrupt halt as his glance fell upon an elderly man seated at his desk.

"What the hell are you doing here?" he demanded angrily.

Deputy Andy Taft, sweat shining on his red face, brushed at his trailing mustache. The thin line of his sandy brows lifted slightly.

"Ease off, son. Don't let this here job get you down."

"Not just a job," Henry said quietly. "Means more than you can guess."

"Maybe so, but I couldn't see no reason for laying around my shack."

Wade pulled off his hat, mopped at his forehead. "You're like some of the others — you

50

don't want to get your head blowed off but you're not willing to help me keep it from happening."

Taft's thin shoulders stirred. "Reckon I'm as good off setting right here as in my place. And could be I can give you a hand, was you to need it."

Henry stared at the older man for a long moment. "Have it your way," he said in resignation.

The deputy heaved himself out of the chair, moved toward the doorway. "Expect they're all giving you fits."

"Yeager, mostly. Seems to think I ought to have the killer locked up by now. And Brock's drunk — drowning himself in whiskey."

"Rufe's that way. Bottle's always been his answer to a problem. How's Kline taking it?"

"Don't seem to be bothered much. I figure he'll do what he's told. It's the others that bother me."

"Seen you visiting them. You chase that drifter out somewhere down the way?"

"The old printing shop. Forbes is missing."

Taft, leaning against the door frame, again tugged at his mustache. "Missing?"

"Not at his place. Didn't run into him anywhere else in town."

"Funny. Ain't nobody else seen him?"

"Yeager's the only one I talked to about

it. Said he hadn't seen him but reckoned he was out looking over some land. If he rode off it was plenty early — before light. I was up by then and I didn't notice him."

The old deputy continued to toy with his mustache. After a time he said, "You figure it means something?"

Wade shook his head, resting himself against the desk. "No way of knowing — yet. I keep remembering he just moved into town a month ago."

"Might mean something at that, but it sure is hard to figure a dandy high-tone like him being hooked up somehow with the likes of them scrubby Dolans."

"With the old man, yes, but how about the woman? You know much about her? She might have come from a better class of people."

"And this here Forbes could be some kin to her — a brother maybe. That what you're driving at?"

"Came to mind."

"Sure could be it," Taft murmured, running a bony finger around the inside of his sodden collar. "Never done no talking to her, howsomeever. Don't think nobody else around here ever did either. She wasn't one to show herself in town. Was always the old man and them two boys that come in — which weren't often."

Henry pulled himself erect and moved to the water bucket standing on a table in the corner of the room. Taking up the tin dipper, he helped himself to a drink and then stood there idly drumming on the bottom of the long-handled cup.

"You aiming to do something about Forbes?" Taft asked.

"Not much I can do except keep an eye on him, and I can't do that until he gets back. Wrong time to leave town and go hunting for him."

"No harm done was he the one we're wanting."

"That's the answer — we don't know that he is. And if he's not, the real killer'll be showing up soon, which means I've got to be here. Won't be any help to you and the others if I'm off somewhere in the hills."

Taft walked lazily back to the desk, perching himself upon its edge. Somewhere over along the creek where the better homes had been built a dog began to bark.

" 'Pears to me, was this here killer just now riding in, he'd a done it last night. Can't figure him waltzing in here while it's broad daylight, for everybody in town to take a squint at. He'd know folks'd be watching for him."

"Way I see it, too. I'm guessing he's here — maybe not right under our noses, but he's close by so's he can ease in when he's ready without anybody noticing. Reason I'm heading out now for a look along the creek and the river. Plenty of places in that brush where a man could hole-up."

"For a fact," Taft agreed. "Now, if you want to stay here I can take me a sashay —"

"You're the one who's staying here!" Henry snapped. "How many times do I have to tell you?"

Andy Taft grunted, reached into a hip pocket for his plug of tobacco. "Wouldn't be knowing that, but this here being a deputy sure don't mean much if you ain't aiming to let me do no deputying."

"We cleared all that up yesterday. You're keeping out of it — staying out of sight same as all the others. Expect there's only one killer we're up against, so one lawman ought to be enough."

"Was thinking last night," the old deputy went on as if not hearing, "we could sort of use me for bait. Stake me out somehow and suck the killer into coming after me first off. That'd —"

Wade Henry reached for a short-barreled shotgun in the wall rack. Breaking it, he slipped shells into its twin chambers and thrust a half a dozen more into a pocket.

"Not using you or anybody else for bait,"

he said, flipping the weapon closed with a jerk of his hand. "I'll get him, but not that way."

Taft was studying the younger man narrowly, his small, dark eyes bright. "Nailing that killer is mighty important to you, ain't it? More'n usual, I mean."

"It is," Henry replied, and let it drop there. "Now, before I go I want it understood you're to stay inside this office."

"Pretty hot —"

"Liable to be a damn sight hotter for you if you show up out there in the street. And keep back from that door — quit standing in it. If you need some air, open up the back for a few minutes. Hear?"

"I hear," Taft mumbled. "You say you're heading out for a look-see along the creek?"

"And the river. Few places I want to check."

The deputy bobbed his head. "Just might run onto something, for sure. Now, there's a old shack back up behind the church. Pretty nigh hid in the brush. Be smart to take a gander at it. And there's the Dolan place. Ain't nobody living in it, far as I know. Killer could be hanging out there."

Wade gave that consideration. The Dolan homestead was some distance from the settlement, however. It would take a couple of hours, at least, to swing by, and he was reluctant to be absent from town for any length of time.

"I'll think about it," he said, moving for the doorway. "Mind what I told you now. Don't go wandering out into the street."

Taft shrugged, biting into his chew. "You're calling the shots," he said. "Have a care."

7

Henry cut back to the stable behind the Enterprise, where he kept his horse. He would have preferred to board the chestnut gelding at Kline's because of the better care he would receive, but the hotel's facilities were handier, being only a few yards from the jail and his own living quarters.

Entering the fairly small building, used mostly for patrons of the hostelry, he sought out the chestnut, threw his gear into place, and in a moment was in the saddle. The hotel maintained a spare-time hostler but Wade saw no sign of him.

Doubling along the south wall of the Enterprise, Henry halted when he reached the street. He let his gaze rake the board walks and storefronts on either side. Two women had ventured forth. Prim in their gingham sunbonnets, they were hurrying toward Yeager's. Aside from their presence, the same hushed restraint still gripped Coyote Springs.

Satisfied, the lawman retraced his path along

the two-story Enterprise and bore directly west for the creek and the scatter of homes, dominated by the larger structures owned by George Yeager and Pete Drum, that had been built among the trees along the stream.

The dog he had heard earlier was now silent, and as he angled the gelding for the house at the extreme end of the grove — Yeager's — he saw a woman come out onto the long verandah. She paused, giving him distant contemplation, and then turned and reentered the structure. Yeager's wife, he supposed.

Moving in closer, he circled the well-tended yard, paying particular attention to the area behind. Seeing nothing of unusual interest, he rode on, pointing now for the residence of Pete Drum, a few hundred feet farther up the stream.

Drum's home, only slightly smaller than Yeager's, had a fair-sized vegetable garden spread beyond it but fewer flowers than its neighbor. A short-legged dog roused from his place beneath the back porch, and hackles erect, sauntered out to greet him. Wade, paying the animal scant heed, completed his survey of the premises and continued on his way.

The same oppressive stillness that claimed the town proper lay upon the area, and as he walked the gelding slowly along the grassy paths and barely defined roads that linked the dozen or so houses, Wade was conscious of the fear that possessed the womenfolk of the settlement, realizing it was no less intense than that being experienced by the men.

The small shack where Andy Taft dwelled came into his vision and there he took time to dismount. He had his look inside as well as doing a thorough investigation of the brush and trees that surrounded it. Again he discovered nothing of unusual note and so moved on, continuing his inspection of the remaining structures built along the meandering stream's course.

The last in the string was occupied by Hugo Kline and his family. Making a slow, careful circuit of the place, he caught sight of several faces beyond the windows, all of which regarded him with an interest akin to suspicion.

He gave it little thought, pleased that all were following his instructions to remain indoors and not tempt the killer to take a hostage by moving about in the open. But it was still early. By noon the heat would begin to tell, and confinement become unbearable. Children and adults alike would turn restless. . . . But it could all be over by then.

He halted a distance north of Kline's, eyes settling upon a giant, spreading cottonwood. Here was where the lynchings had taken place. Jeb Dolan and his sons, Hughie and Dan, had been strung up side by side from one of the stout lower limbs. It was strange irony that the town's only church and its adjoining graveyard lay but a dozen strides farther on.

The Dolans had not been accorded burial there, however. Sometime during the night following the hanging, unknown parties had cut down the bodies, wrapped them in blankets, and taken them to the Dolan farm. Henry winced as he visualized the moment when the unheralded Samaritans had driven into the homestead yard and delivered to the Dolan woman the lifeless figures of her menfolk. She had buried them herself, he supposed; no one seemed to know for sure. A month or so later she too was dead. Shock, or perhaps a broken heart — and there were a few who said it was starvation.

No matter, there was nothing to be gained by thinking of it. The terrible act had been done, and the Dolans were out of it. Now vengeance rode the stifling hot air, and the threats of an avenger no one could comprehend was poised, like a Damoclean sword, over the entire settlement.

That retribution might be justified was out of the question. To some it was, but another wrong in the shape of more killings and a fiery torch would not right the original transgression. It had to end where it now stood, and the responsibility for seeing to it was his.

Henry stirred, pulling his unseeing eyes from the motionless cottonwood, quiet and enduring in the blazing sunlight. It was a pleasant place except for the stain of memory. Grass covered the shaded ground, and there were occasional clumps of purple verbena, white-petaled cowslips, and wild marigold. The muttering creek, hemmed by dogwood and willow, was dappled by overhanging branches as it flowed ceaselessly on.

But here the witchery ended. The numbing silence touched all, leaving the beauty lifeless and turning even the meadowlarks and the clamorous jays mute.

The lawman roweled the chestnut with his spurs and slanted him toward the cemetery with its collection of staggering headboards and weathered stone markers. Circling the low fence that surrounded the plot, he came in to the side of the church and dismounted.

Stepping up to the door quietly, he opened it and entered. The narrow, hall-like structure was filled with breathless heat. He saw no one, but taking nothing for granted, and cradling the scattergun loosely in his arms, he walked the length of the building, looking carefully between the rows of wooden benches that served as pews.

Convinced there was no one hiding in the

sanctuary, Wade returned to the chestnut. He paused, seeing the lean figure of the Reverend Daily bearing down upon him from the nearby parsonage. He nodded his greeting as the minister approached, and then went to the saddle.

"Yes, Marshal?"

"Just having a look around — for strangers," Henry replied.

Daily's long face was immobile. "It is doubtful you will find such a man as you search for here."

"Could be the most likely place he'd choose to hide. Seen anybody riding by you didn't know?"

The minister rubbed dry soil from his hands. Evidently he had been interrupted while toiling in his garden. "No, I have not."

"If you do," the lawman said, wiping sweat from his face, "I'll appreciate your getting word to me." He hesitated, pointed to the belfry of the church. "Maybe it would be better to start ringing your bell. I'll know right off what it means."

Daily said, "Yes, that will be better. Marshal, do you really think someone will come, do all the things that letter said?"

Henry shrugged. "Who knows for sure? Up to me to figure there will be."

The minister's eyes settled on the shotgun

laid across Wade's lap. A worn frown pulled at his features.

"It is a terrible thing — a thing that has no end. One man hunting another like some wild beast, and intending only to kill. There is no respect for the sanctity of life."

"Not a matter of wanting to, Reverend. Case of stopping him before he can kill someone else — several, in fact."

"I know, but is there justification —"

"Was no good reason for those lynchings, either, but they happened. This is what comes afterwards — and I'm trying to keep the score from getting bigger, I'm not out looking for a man just to shoot him down."

Daily looked off into the valley. "I suppose you're right, only we're taught that killing is wrong and we should believe it. There is another way, a better way —"

"Expect there is, but I reckon it hasn't reached this part of the country yet. Be obliged if you'll keep your eyes open for strangers."

"Yes, yes, of course," the minister said, and stepped back as Wade headed the gelding out of the yard.

The shack. . . . He'd almost forgotten it, Henry realized. He had been somewhat nettled by his conversation with Daily. Abruptly he cut the chestnut hard left and rode straight for the deeper brush on the slope beyond the creek.

Fording the stream, he pulled the horse down to a slow walk, muffling the big gelding's hoof beats in the soft mat of decaying leaves and grass that covered the dark earth.

He soon located the shack and halted in a thicket to study it closely. There appeared to be no one around, and presently he closed in and swung from the saddle. Shotgun leveled, he made his way through the undergrowth, walking quietly and deliberately, ears and eyes attuned to the moment.

The slab door of the disintegrating hut was hanging from one leather hinge. Edging to one side, Wade tried to see inside from the cover of the brush, but all was dark within and he could obtain no satisfactory look at the interior. Stalling out another minute, he abruptly moved forward, and gun ready, stepped through the doorway.

The shack was empty. Back to a wall, he stared about as his eyes became adjusted to the gloom in the heat-laden structure. No one had been there for months, he would guess, judging from the loose dust that covered the floor.

Wheeling, Henry pushed back through the doorway, crossed to the chestnut, and swinging aboard, pressed on, pointing now for the grove bordering the east edge of the settlement where the Coyote River cut its direct path toward the south.

Breaking out of the last of the trees beyond the church, he slowed the gelding to a halt. Dust was rising on the road that came in from the north, and studying the tan boil intently he made out several riders and a spring wagon pointing for town.

A coldness slipped through him, and immediately he roweled the chestnut into a fast lope. Slicing diagonally through the thinning trees and clumps of rabbitbush, he rode in ahead of the party and pulled to a stop. It was Ed Cameron, foreman of Code's J-Bar-C ranch, with several of his riders.

A moment later the tautness that gripped him gave way to a heavy-hearted grimness when he saw the canvas-shrouded body in the wagon.

8

The lawman's eyes shifted to the sullen-faced riders, and came to a halt on the stolid Cameron.

"Code?" he asked, knowing the answer.

The J-Bar-C foreman's weathered features were like granite. "It's him."

Wade Henry settled back into his saddle as the heaviness within him increased. All the precautions he had taken, all the careful planning, had been for nothing. The killer had struck, claimed his first victim.

"Mind telling me what happened?"

"He got plugged, that's what!" one of the punchers said angrily. "You're the law, you ought've —"

Anger whipped through Henry. The attitude of the J-Bar-C men seemed to be that he was solely to blame for the rancher's death.

"I ought to what? Wet nurse him?" he cut in. "Hell, there are five more men mixed up in this — and Code was warned to be careful, same as they've been."

"He was the one that bastard wanted most — it being his cows that was getting rustled. You ought've figured that, spent your time watching out for —"

"Never mind, Maje," Cameron said, lifting his hand. "Ain't no hay getting cut by bitching now. Jess's dead and arguing ain't apt to bring him back."

Henry put his attention once more on the foreman. "Asking you again, how'd it happen?"

"Some jasper with a rifle. Was hiding in them rocks south of the house."

Henry frowned, recalling the Code ranch and its surroundings. The buttes Cameron mentioned were a considerable distance from the house. A man would need to be an excellent marksman to kill at that range.

"Jess must've come out, like he's been doing every morning for years, to have himself a look at the weather —"

"When was that?"

"About sun-up, I reckon. Maybe a bit before. He was just standing there, I expect, when this bird cut down on him from the rocks. Killed him dead first shot."

The lawman thought for a few moments. Then, "Way you tell, there wasn't anybody else around."

"Wasn't — not close, anyway. We was all in the bunkhouse, mostly. Was some of the boys eating breakfast. Hardly nobody heard anything."

Henry nodded. "Can understand that. Man holed up in those rocks would've had himself a long shot."

"What I was thinking. It'd take a mighty good shooter."

"You look for the killer?"

Cameron spat. "Why, hell yes! What'd you think we'd do? The boss was laying there already dead when we got to him, which was maybe a couple of minutes after that bullet got him. I weren't sure where the bushwhacker'd been hiding. Could've just rode right into the yard, far as I knew, 'cause, like I said, we was all around in the back.

"So, I had a bunch of the boys saddle up quick and start beating the brush. Never turned up nobody. Was later on when I was poking around in them rocks myself that I come across a empty cartridge. Nothing special about it. Expect there's a hundred rifles in this valley using the same kind."

"No tracks?"

"Plenty, but there's so much coming and going around here that a man couldn't tell nothing from them," Cameron said, pulling off his hat and mopping the back of his neck.

"I figure he knowed that, and run his horse right over the tracks that'd been made by others."

"Whoever he was," Maje said, "he sure did get out of the country awful fast. We started hunting him quick. I know, 'cause I was one of the bunch that done it."

Wade stared out across the valley. "The first one," he murmured.

"What's that?" Cameron asked sharply.

"Was thinking Code's the first one on the list to get killed. I'm wondering who's next in line."

"Well, they're goners if you don't do no better job looking out for them than you did for Jess," Maje said, sarcastically.

Temper again lifted in Henry, but he shrugged it off. "Only so much I can do — or anybody else for that matter. Rode out and talked to Code yesterday. Warned him to be careful, stay inside his house so's I could force the killer into the open —"

"The boss weren't the kind to crawl in a hole — not for nobody —"

"Pity he wasn't — at least for this one time. Maybe he wouldn't be laying there wrapped in a tarp. Rest of the men named in that letter are listening to me and keeping out of sight. None of them like doing it either, but they know it's the only way I can get to that killer

69

before he gets to them."

"Well, Jess wasn't like them counter-jumpers in town. He was a real, honest-to-God man."

"And now he's a dead one."

Ed Cameron mulled that over in silence. Finally, he said, "You aiming to ride out to the ranch and look around?"

"No use. Said you'd already scouted the country and found nothing."

"Still are. Got a dozen of the boys right now combing the hills and arroyos."

"Expect they're wasting their time. That killer won't be hanging around. He was long gone before you ever got your men saddled up and on the move. Right now he'll be somewhere close to town, looking for a chance to slip in, nail somebody else."

Cameron scrubbed at the sweaty stubble on his chin. "Maybe you're right, but we'll keep looking just in case — and if we roast out some jaybird, we aim to have us a rope party right then and there —"

"And start another killing on the way," the lawman said wearily. "If you find somebody, you bring him to me; let me handle it. Code and the others taking the law into their own hands is what put this town in the fix it's in today. Remember that."

"We're only remembering that some

sonofabitch potshot Jess," Maje muttered. "And we ain't forgetting it until we got him hanging from a tree."

Wade Henry shrugged. "Guess you're one of those who never learns," he said, and shifted attention to Cameron.

"Be obliged to you if you'll swing around town and come into Schmitt's from the back so's you won't be seen hauling Code's body in. Town's spooked bad enough without them knowing he's been murdered. Like for you to tell Schmitt to keep it quiet, too."

The J-Bar-C foreman, some of the hostility gone from his manner, bobbed his head. "All the same to me," he said, and wheeled his horse about to face the men behind him. "You heard the marshal. We ain't advertising that the boss is dead. Want you all to keep it under your hat. Ain't right to make a man's job no harder'n it already is, and I reckon his is plenty tough."

Wade watched the men ride off in silence, the thought running through his mind that there could be no doubt now, not in anyone's mind, that the letter was far from a joke; there was a killer — and he was there. It was only a matter of time before he would single out and claim another on his list — unless he could be found and stopped.

Spurring the chestnut, Henry moved on,

pointing now for the deep grove of trees along the Coyote River on the eastern edge of the settlement. The area, well brushed over, offered ideal cover for a man wishing to keep out of sight, and there were no homes there to avoid.

He glanced ahead to the dark band of growth as he back-handed the sweat from his face. The ride could be for nothing; chances were good the killer was now inside the settlement, having slipped in sometime after he had lain in wait for Jess Code and downed him with an accurately placed bullet. If true, the chances were also good that someone had noticed his arrival, since all had been warned to be on the alert.

But he'd take a turn through the grove anyway, and be certain. Then he would return to town and make the rounds again.

9

Wade Henry turned into the dusty street and rode slowly down its center for his office at the far end. The search through the grove had proved fruitless; nor were there any indications that there had been any recent camps.

He let his glance swing to the building that housed Schmitt's Undertaking Parlor, noting that the spring wagon Cameron and the J-Bar-C riders had used in bringing Jess Code's body to town was still there along with their horses. The punchers were not in evidence, however. It was likely they were inside the nearby Alamo Saloon drenching their somber moods with whiskey. He'd hoped that once arrangements were made with Schmitt, the riders would head back to the ranch; the possibility of word of Code's death leaking out would thereby have been greatly decreased.

There was little change along the street. The same blistering heat, the same leaden silence, the same furtive faces peering from windows. . . . But there was a change in him. The killer was there, and could at that exact moment be watching him from one of the passageways that separated the buildings or from some other place of concealment; that awareness stiffened the tension within him, causing a prickling along his spine.

A lone horse stood at Yeager's hitchrack, and down in front of the Enterprise a man stepped out onto the gallery, glanced briefly about, and ducked back hastily into the bulking building.

As he drew abreast the general store, Wade took note of the horse. The brand was unfamiliar. He slowed, raised his eyes to the glass pane. Beyond it he could see Yeager in conversation with a stranger clad in ordinary range clothing. Henry frowned, swore harshly. He had cautioned the storekeeper to stay well back from the window; his words were having little effect, just as they had fallen on deaf ears where Jess Code was concerned.

Disgust and impatience filling him, he continued on down the street, a rigid, square-shouldered shape in the saddle, now looking to neither right nor left. Coming to the jail, he veered to the sycamore that grew in the lot behind it and brought the chestnut to a halt. He'd leave the horse there where it would be ready for instant use, he had decided.

Slinging the shotgun under his arm, he

moved back to the front of the building and entered. Taft had watched him ride in, and now stood in the center of the heat-packed room, waiting.

"Can see something's gone wrong —"

Henry propped the gun against a wall and pulled off his hat. "Jess Code — he's dead."

The old deputy's jaw snapped shut. After a moment he wagged his head. "Might've knowed he'd be the first one."

"And Yeager'll be the next!" Henry snapped. "Why the hell can't they do what I tell them? He's standing down there in his window right now — just asking that killer to put a bullet in him!"

"Like as not it just slipped his mind," Taft said gently. "George ain't anxious to die."

"Probably slipped Code's mind, too. Got him killed. Can't expect me to keep them alive if they won't listen to me!"

"No, they sure can't," the deputy said. "And you're a dang fool if you blame yourself when they don't. You been out to Code's?"

"Ran into Cameron and some of the crew bringing Code's body in to Schmitt."

"They get a look at who done it?"

"No," Wade said, dropping into a chair. Sweat was glistening on his browned skin, and the upper area of his shirt was dark where it had soaked through. "Killer picked him off from those rocks south of the house when he stepped outside. Cameron and the whole bunch scouted the country good. He'd already gone."

"Reckon we couldn't expect much else. He'd a got out of there fast," Taft said, loosening his shirt front. "This goddam heat's fierce — and the day's hardly started." He hesitated, stared out through the open doorway. "Well, reckon that means all hell's going to bust loose around here now. Whoever it is'll be making another move pretty quick. . . . You didn't turn up nobody in the woods?"

The lawman stirred tiredly. "Nobody; no sign anywhere. That shack you told me about — hasn't seen a visitor in months. Everything been quiet around here?"

"Worse'n that. It's like the town was dead. Be worse, too, soon's word gets out that Code's been shot."

"Had the J-Bar-C outfit take the body to Schmitt's the back way. Told them to keep it quiet."

"Ain't much hope of that. It'll leak out somehow."

"Probably, but I've got to try and keep the lid on things somehow, spooked as everyone is. . . . You know a man they call Maje that works for Jess Code?"

"Sure. Clint Majors."

"Was plenty worked up over the killing. Sort of blamed me for letting it happen."

"That's Maje, all right. Got hisself a big, flapping mouth. How the hell could he fault you for it? You're doing all you can."

"Been wondering about that," Henry said thoughtfully. "I've asked myself if I've missed anything — but I can't see what. How long has Maje worked for the J-Bar-C?"

"Year, could be a bit more." The deputy fixed his eyes on Henry. "You thinking maybe he could have something to do with killing Jess?"

Wade shifted on the chair. "Not especially. Just seemed to me he was doing a lot of talking. Cameron shut him up a couple of times."

Taft shook his head. "Don't see's how he could be mixed up in it. He'd be all for Code's side of the thing."

"Unless he had a grudge against Code and jumped at the chance to use that letter the killer wrote as a cover-up to even a score."

"You mean he'd be getting his licks in but folks'd think it was the killer?"

"Farfetched, and I'm not saying there's anything to it," Henry said, "but I'm looking at everything — and everybody."

"Including me?"

The lawman cocked his head to one side. "Could be you at that," he said, smiling. "Understand you wanted this job, but Yeager and the town council didn't give it to you. Maybe you're getting back at them. . . . And you didn't show up here early this morning. You could've ridden out to Code's, shot him, and had time to get back."

Andy Taft was staring at Wade. "You meaning all that for true or are you just funning?"

"Just funning," Henry replied. "Telling you that because before this day's over somebody's likely to come up with what I told you and start asking questions. Everybody's going to be a suspect — even me."

"You? How the hell —"

"Why not? Sooner or later some fool's going to remember that I blew in here a little over a month ago, and come up with the idea that it was me that wrote the letter and is out to get even for the Dolans. Being the marshal, it'd be easy for me to do it."

"And jumpy as the town is, plenty of folks'll swallow it! By damn, you got me thinking slanchwise, now. Don't know what to figure."

"One thing," Henry said. "That letter was no joke. First man's dead, just like it promised. Somebody else on the list will be next, and there's no way of guessing who it'll be. I've got to forget the side possibilities and start putting my mind on them, and the only way

I know to do that is walk the street — and watch."

"Only way," Taft agreed solemnly. "You aim to tell George and the others about Code?"

"Have to," the lawman said, rising. "Best they know what's happened. Could make them harken to me, be a bit more careful. Code would be alive right now if he'd bent a little, stayed out of sight. Instead he walks right out into the open, gives the killer a perfect target."

"Jess always was one for doing what he pleased."

"This time it cost him his life. . . . You seen Forbes come in yet?"

Andy Taft shook his head. "If'n he did, he didn't come by this way. Doubt if he has. Quiet as everything is, I'd heard him sure."

Wade stared out into the glaring sunlight. "Would give a lot to know where he went."

"Would be mighty interesting," the old deputy said, rubbing at his jaw. "I ain't doing no good here. Could catch up my horse and take a *pasear* down the valley, see if I can spot him. Be nobody see me, was I right careful."

"Forget it. Be running too big a risk. We've got no idea which way he went, anyway."

Taft swore. "Well, I sure am getting powerful tired of being cooped up like a damn chicken —"

Henry raised a hand for silence. "Now, don't you go giving me trouble! Getting enough of that from some of the others — and I sure wouldn't like having you toted over to Schmitt's for a boxing. Besides, hot as it is in here, it's a damn sight hotter out there in the sun."

Taft grinned humorlessly, moved back to the desk, and settled into the chair behind it. "Reckon you're right. You've got enough riding your back now without me making it worse. Where you going now?"

"Back into the street."

"Wish't I could help —"

"Could use it, but putting you out there would be the same as standing you up in a shooting gallery for that killer to take a crack at."

"Seems you're plenty sure he's right here in town now."

"Makes sense. After he shot Code, the next thing he'd do would be to come here and get himself squared away for the second man on the list. Just hoping I can find somebody who saw him when he got here."

Picking up the shotgun, Henry crossed to the door. He paused, leveling his eyes at the deputy. "There anything you can think of I'm overlooking?"

Taft nodded. "Yes sir, one thing. While you're doing your parading up and down worrying about them others getting shot, you're setting yourself up real handylike for a bullet in the back, too."

Wade Henry smiled bleakly. "There any other way to do it?" he asked, and stepped out into the blazing sunlight.

10

Cradling the shotgun, Henry stood motionless in the brilliant glare, his glance slowly, methodically, probing along the buildings that fronted the slightly curving dust strip.

Again the awareness that he had experienced earlier was with him, tightening his muscles, sharpening his nerves as it laid its close caution upon him. It was not a fear for his own well-being; death was an incidental factor, never relished, but encountered by a man in one form or another during almost every day of his life.

Rather, it was a dread that his efforts to protect the men who had entrusted him with their lives would fall short, and in failing them he would again fail himself.

And there was no avoiding the fact that now he, too, was the killer's enemy and likely marked for a bullet just the same as those who had been involved in the Dolan lynchings. Long before, at the time when he had accepted the task, he had faced that possibility and deemed it worth the risk. Coyote Springs was the end of the line insofar as finding himself was concerned; here his future would rise or else be buried in the powdery dust of the street.

His jaw taut, Wade Henry moved on, walking at a deliberate pace, eyes whipping back and forth touching the narrow, dark oblongs of the passageway entries, the windows and doors of the silent buildings — even the roofs and corners of their false fronts. It was as if he were alone in a deserted, long-forgotten town.

He reached the Enterprise Hotel and angled toward its entrance. Gaining it, he stepped into the small, stuffy lobby. Moisture clouded his vision. Brushing it away irritably, he continued on to the connecting archway, with its heavy, sagging portieres, which led into the saloon and casino.

Halting, he glanced about the large, shadowy room. The three women who worked for Drum, dressed in their usual gaudy finery, were at the bar talking with the apronman behind it. There were no customers.

"Where's Pete?" he called

One of the girls stirred languidly, motioning in the direction of the café. Wade turned, made his way to that adjoining area. Drum was seated at a back table staring moodily into a cup of coffee. He looked up as the lawman entered. Hope sprang into his eyes.

Henry shook his head. "Code's dead," he said flatly.

The light in Pete Drum's eyes faded instantly. He groaned, settling deeper into his chair. "How?"

"Walked out into his yard early this morning. Somebody picked him off with a rifle."

"Somebody? The killer, you're meaning."

Wade's shoulders stirred. "Nobody else gunning for him that I know of."

"Means he's here," the hotelman said nervously.

"Sure of it. Hiding somewhere in town."

Drum mustered a tired grin. "Town ain't so big a place that he'll find many spots to hole up. You figure there's a chance you can root him out?"

"Good chance. I'm keeping Code's death quiet. Telling only you and Yeager and the others on the list so's you'll be more careful. I'd as soon the rest of the town don't know about it."

"Won't get past me," Drum said. "Figure I might as well close up, anyway, for all the business I'm doing. Sort of like we're the only people in town."

"That's how I'd like it to stay until I can get that killer behind bars," Henry said, and turned for the door.

Once more on the street, he gave it sharp scrutiny and moved on, walking fairly close to the building fronts, exposing himself no more than necessary. Directly across from Yeager's at that point, he could see in and was relieved to note the storekeeper was well back inside and no longer framed in the window as he had been earlier. The lone patron and his horse were gone.

Abreast Sutton's, Henry glanced into the small partitioned area in the front, crowded by its display case and stock shelves. He saw neither Willa nor Burl. Likely he was upstairs working in his shop; Willa would be straightening their living quarters in the rear, or perhaps preparing the noon meal.

The shades of Miss Camille's dress shop were now raised. Inside, the tall, elderly woman was in conversation with another female — a customer no doubt. Wade smiled grimly. Despite the paralysis that gripped the town, the planning for a new frock must go on.

He found Hugo Kline mending a harness in the back area of the barn, and told him of Jess Code's death. The old Quaker shook his head sadly.

"He was a fool to pay thee no heed, Marshal. And for being a fool a man must pay a price.

But I am sorry for him."

"Means the killer's banging around here now," Henry continued. "Seen anybody about you didn't know?"

The stable owner said, "We have watched, Marshal, the hostler and the boy and me. A few have come to trade at the stores. All were people who live here. They come and they go quickly."

Wade wheeled to leave, then paused. "Not letting out the word that Code's dead. Better if the town in general doesn't know — only you and Yeager and the others."

"I understand," Kline said in his melancholy way.

Wade next checked the building in which he had found Texas Jack Kincaid. It was empty, stifling with trapped heat. He passed on to Zakowski's and then to Arky's saloon. Both men declared they had noticed no strangers either entering or leaving town.

"Only thing I've seen," the saloonman said, "was a bunch from the J-Bar-C. Had a wagon. Come in for supplies, I reckon."

"Could be. Appreciate your still keeping your eyes open," the lawman had said, and crossed the sun-struck street to Simon's.

He encountered no better luck there or at the Star Café. Wayland's note that he was out on a call was still pinned to the door, and he by-passed Schmitt's, knowing the man, busy inside his gloomy, cavernlike place, would have been paying no attention to the outside world.

He halted in front of the Alamo Saloon, watching as a man and woman came from the vacant lot between Kline's and Miss Camille's and hurried toward Yeager's. Their movements were furtive, as if being seen on the street was unlawful and they hoped, by haste, to go unseen. . . . But it was fear of danger, not of the law, that prompted their actions.

Scanning the street further, Wade came about and started up onto the porch of the Alamo, noting as he did that Cameron and his riders were no longer present.

"Morning again, Marshal," Cook drawled from the doorway. "Still a hunting your killer?"

Wade halted, nodding. "Was hoping you'd have some word for me —"

"About seeing somebody I don't know? Sure ain't. Quiet as the boneyard around here."

Henry bobbed his head, dropped back to the walk, and pressed on, following his pattern of keeping close to the walls while his eyes continually raked the hot, silent street.

He pulled up abruptly at the corner of the saloon. A horse stood at the rack in the rear of Forbes' building. The land broker, absent earlier, had returned. The tautness within him suddenly increasing, Wade circled to the back door of the structure and halted. Forbes' voice reached out to him at once.

"Come in, come in, Marshal — out of that heat!"

The lawman stepped into the room, only a little less hot than the outside. Shoulders to the wall, he studied the man for a long moment. Then, "You just ride in?"

Forbes, boots off, a drink of some kind in his hand, was sitting in a rocking chair. His forehead knitted into a frown. "Fifteen, twenty minutes ago. Why?"

"Was by here before. You weren't around."

"Rode out to look over a piece of property I'm thinking of buying."

"Whose?"

"The Finley place," the land broker said, his brow again wrinkling. Leaning forward he set his glass on the table close by. "There something on your mind?"

"Only questions. You talk to Finley?"

A faint smile of amusement pulled at Forbes' lips. "No, matter of fact, I didn't. Matters haven't reached that point. Was mainly interested in getting the lay of the land. What's this all about?"

Henry made no answer, giving careful

thought to the man's words. . . . A visit to a ranch several miles east of town — one in which he'd not bothered to talk with the owner.

"Just getting things straight in my head," he said finally.

The bland smile on the land broker's face persisted. He shrugged, settled back. "Of course," he murmured. "It's about that gunman that everyone's expecting. You're trying to keep folks in one place so you will know where they are."

"Something like that. You run into anybody while you were going or coming?"

"Well, no. Did see a couple in a buggy driving toward town. Wasn't close enough to recognize them. Are you making any progress in finding the murderer?"

The lawman's eyes narrowed. "Murderer?"

"Yes — Jess Code's. Too bad about him."

Henry considered the land broker quietly. Word of the rancher's death was still a secret, one known so far only to Taft, Pete Drum, Kline, and, of course, the J-Bar-C outfit and the undertaker — and they had been warned to keep it to themselves.

"How'd you know about Code?" he asked coldly.

Carson Forbes frowned, wiped his face with

a white handkerchief. "Why, I heard it in the saloon, I guess. The Alamo."

Wade's thoughts swung back to the moments just before when he had spoken with Cook, the owner of the saloon. The Texan had made no mention of the rancher's killing.

"Dropped in there when I got back," Forbes said. "Little habit of mine, dropping by and fixing myself a drink. Don't like bar whiskey. Mix myself a concoction of rye and bourbon, laced with beer. Was while I was doing that I heard some of Code's men talking about it. I believe they said it was somebody hiding in the rocks."

Henry made no comment. He waited, features stolid and unrevealing.

"Have you any idea who the murderer might be?" Forbes continued, again placing his question, but in slightly different words.

"A hunch. Not much more than that," the lawman replied, breaking his silence. "You aim to stay in town the rest of the day?"

Forbes took up his glass again. "Was planning to look at another piece of land —"

"Best you forget it — wait."

Carson Forbes frowned, stared at Henry. "Are you ordering me not to leave?"

"No. Only telling you it would be better to hold off until things settle down a bit."

The broker nodded. "I see. Well, I did

promise, and I like to keep my word when I do. I'll give it some thought." He took a sip of his drink. "Appreciate your worrying over my safety, however."

Wade Henry watched the man brush beads of moisture from his neatly trimmed mustache with a slender forefinger. If Forbes was the killer he was a cool one, and plenty smooth.

"Sure don't want anything happening to you," he said, matching the broker's misconceived idea concerning his personal security with equally erroneous words, and wheeling about, stepped back into the yard.

Retracing his path along the building, he returned to the Alamo and entered its dim interior. Cook, standing behind his plank counter wiping glasses, looked up questioningly.

"Something bring you back —"

"Was Forbes in here a few minutes ago — when the J-Bar-C bunch was around?"

The lean Texan bobbed his head. "Reckon he was. Mixed up one of them fancy drinks of his'n. Why?"

"Claims he heard some of the riders talking about Jess Code. You hear it?"

"Did, for a fact. But they said to keep it under my hat and I'm doing it."

"You didn't mention it to me when I dropped by."

Cook shrugged. "Like I said, was told not to talk about it — and you already was knowing so there weren't no sense bringing it up. Why? That there dude spill it to somebody? Warned him to keep his jaw shut."

Henry pulled off his hat and ran his fingers through his shock of damp hair. That much of Carson Forbes' story was true; the part concerning the Finleys was yet to be verified. That would be hard to do since the land broker had stated he talked with no one, had seen only an unknown couple at an unrecognizable distance. If he —

"Marshal — Marshal!"

Wade Henry pivoted at the cry coming from the street. He gained the door in a dozen long strides, then burst out onto the gallery.

"Anybody seen the marshal? Somebody's killed Rufe Brock — stabbed him!"

11

10:35 A.M.

Henry plunged off the Alamo's porch and
ran toward the man standing in front of the
feed store. People were appearing in doorways along the dusty strip — old Zakowski,
a boot in one hand, peg hammer in the other,
Kline's hostler, Forbes, Miss Camille with
Willa at her side while Burl Sutton looked
down from his window above, and a few others.

Relief flooded through him when he saw
that none of the remaining men on the killer's
list were to be seen; they were heeding his
advice to stay out of sight.

The homesteader, from the looks of his
clothing, moved toward the lawman at a trot.
His hair was long, straggling out from under
the battered straw hat he wore, and his leath-
ery face was strained.

"Was a fork — a pitchfork," he babbled.
"Jabbed Rufe right in the back!"

Drawing abreast and not slowing his pace,

Henry gave the man a sharp glance. "Who're you, mister?"

"Name's Penny. John Penny. Got a farm down the river a piece. Come to see Rufe about some feed — found him laying —"

Wade veered from the center of the street, sped up onto the landing that fronted Brock's, and hurried through the open doorway. He pulled up short. Andy Taft was standing beside the bloody figure of the feed store owner.

"Run over here when I heard Penny yelling," the deputy explained before Henry could speak. "Figured maybe I could get a look at who done it."

The lawman moved up to the body. "Did you?"

The deputy wagged his head "Was too late. Plenty too late, I'd guess. Blood's dried hard. Rufe's been dead most onto an hour, I'd say."

At least that long, Henry thought, touching the crusted stains. An arm's length away lay the fork, the tips of its sharp-pointed tines smeared with brown.

"You pull that out of his back?"

Taft said, "No," and glanced to Penny. "You?"

"No, sir! Never touched nothing. Was just the way you're a seeing when I come walking in the back door."

Wade shifted his attention to the rear of the

long room. He'd told Brock to lock the heavy panel, and if failing to find the key, block it with something.

"You sure you came in through the back?" he asked the homesteader.

"Yes, sir, I am. My team and wagon's out there now, right where I left them."

"It make some kind of difference?" Taft asked, looking into the street. Two of the Enterprise Saloon girls were on the landing, craning their necks as they endeavored to get a better look inside the feed store. Beyond them, standing in the dust, was a small group of men.

"Told Rufe to lock that door. Guess he never got around to doing it."

"The killer would've had to come in that way, else I'd seen him," the deputy said.

Wade nodded absently, eyes on the body at his feet. Two men dead now — two of the six named in the letter. And the murderer was still unknown — loose somewhere in the town. His labored thoughts flipped to Carson Forbes. The man admitted having been out of the settlement when Jess Code was shot — and he could furnish no proof as to where he claimed to have been. Also, Forbes had returned less than an hour ago, unnoticed. He could have ridden in behind Brock's, entered, made use of the pitchfork, and hurried on to his quarters with no one paying any attention to his movements. It all fit nicely — almost too nicely, Wade decided.

Wheeling, he stepped out onto the landing, beckoning to the cluster of hushed men who had moved to in front of Dollarhide's barbershop.

"Some of you come in here. Want you to carry Brock down to Schmitt's."

Three of the party separated from the group, mounted the wooden platform, and filed silently into the feed store.

"Use the alley," Henry said, walking past them to the back door and swinging it open.

The impromptu pallbearers picked up Brock's body, two at the shoulders, one positioning himself between the legs.

"You wanting us to tell the undertaker anything?" one of them asked as they stepped out into the harsh sunlight.

"He knows what to do," Wade answered, and closed the door.

"Reckon that leaves four," Andy Taft said laconically. "I'm wondering who's next."

The lawman crossed the room slowly. "Like to know that myself," he said, continuing on until he reached the window. "Could maybe keep it from happening."

The street was empty again, left to the driving heat and the brittle tension that had leaped to a higher plane with Brock's death. It would grow even worse, for now there'd be no keeping the news of Code's murder a secret.

"Ain't you got no idea at all who it might be?"

Wade Henry thought he detected a note of desperation in the deputy's voice — or could he be mistaking it. Was it, instead, exasperation? Yeager and Drum, and possibly Hugo Kline, would likely be having their doubts concerning him by then, too, he supposed.

He reckoned he couldn't blame them. So far he had failed completely. Two men dead at the hands of the killer — no matter that he had cautioned them, and the warning been ignored — they were dead.

"Hunch — nothing more."

Taft pushed forward hurriedly, his boot heels clacking on the board floor. "Who?"

"Forbes."

The deputy's watery eyes widened. "Him, huh? Been thinking some about him myself —"

"Don't go jumping the gun," Henry said. "Just happens that the way it works out he could've shot Code and he could have been the one that jabbed that hay fork into Rufe. But it's only that he could have — there's no proof that he did."

Taft stroked his long mustache. "It'd fit, it being him. Just moving into town, I mean.

But like we was saying before, why'd he want to do it? Him being hooked up with them Dolans sure don't seem natural."

At the far end of the street the man and woman Wade had watched enter Yeager's store earlier were now hurrying back for Kline's wagonyard, where they had apparently left their transportation. A sudden wave of despair rolled through the lawman.

"Hell, I'm falling flat on my face trying to handle this job," he said "Best thing I can do is see George Yeager, tell him he'd best get somebody else."

"Little late for that," Taft said. He studied Henry for a long moment, then shook his head. "Now, there ain't no use you getting all worked up and blaming yourself. You're doing all any man could do — and that's all anybody's expecting."

"Code and Rufe Brock — they expected more."

"Be alive, too, dammit, if they'd paid some mind to you. How's a man to help if others won't listen?"

Henry mopped at his face. "Seems I ought to have turned up something on the killer by now. Way it adds, I'm no closer to stopping him than I was a week ago."

The deputy's thin shoulders lifted, then fell. "Could be you are, only you can't see it yet.

98

. . . You aiming to do something about Forbes?"

"Watch him — that's about all I can do. If he makes a move that don't look right, I'll lock him up. But I've got to have a reason first."

"Could be he'll give you one. Only four of us left now. Makes it easier for you. More I think about that slicker, the more I get the feeling he's maybe our man."

"Only bet so far," Wade said. "Come on, I'll walk you across to the office. You're not paying any better attention to my warnings than some of the others — running over here the way you did."

Taft dropped his gaze and started for the door. "Reckon I just wasn't thinking. When old John Penny come a yelling out of Rufe's, I just naturally went boiling over there. Plain forgot."

"Which could have been the last time you'd ever forget anything if that killer had still been hanging around close, just hoping you or Yeager or one of the others would show up on the street."

"That's right," the old deputy said as they struck out for the jail, "and it's sort of funny. We know he's here in town somewheres — why do you reckon he didn't up and plug me?"

"Wondered about that, too," Henry said. "Guess he must have a cut-and-dried plan. He's taking it slow and easy, one at a time, making everybody sweat it out. . . . Now, I'm telling you again — stay inside. Don't get sucked out like you just did. Next time it could be your turn."

12

The crippling inertia that now gripped the settlement following Rufe Brock's death was total. It was evident in the deeper hush, in the absence of faces no longer peering from windows.

It was what the killer wanted. His scheme had been one of creating a pall of terror, of paralyzing fright, Henry knew, and thus driving home in the minds of not only those involved in the lynchings, but of the entire town as well, his lesson of bloody retribution.

The lawman had left the shotgun at the jail after seeing Andy Taft safely inside, and now unencumbered by the heavier weapon, right hand riding close to the forty-five strapped to his thigh, he walked slowly along the board strip, constantly probing the street, the passageways, the buildings, and breaking that pattern at times by dropping back to the alleys for a close look.

Once he paused to brush at the sweat clothing his face and swore quietly, helplessly. It was ridiculous to think he could not ferret out the killer in a place so small as Coyote Springs. How could a man move about without being seen by someone? It was as if he were dealing with a ghost.

He moved on at a slow pace, taking each step with calculated deliberateness and never once relaxing his vigilance. The killer's eyes were upon him at that very moment, he was certain, and it was conceivable that he, too, would feel the smashing impact of a bullet. After all, he represented the law and therefore was a threat to the man's plans.

But Wade Henry was not thinking of that; the lives of the remaining four men on the list and the fate of the town occupied his mind, and he was simply gambling that the Dolan family's avenger would ignore him rather than jeopardize the completion of the plan that had already succeeded in part.

He halted in front of the bakery, grateful for the shade of a small tree growing at the edge of the sidewalk. The tension, the silence, the heat, had all combined to increase the oppression that enclosed him, and he was suddenly aware of his own strained breathing.

He shrugged impatiently and took a deep breath, when he caught motion beyond the glass of Yeager's window directly opposite. Looking close he saw that the storekeeper was beckoning to him.

Henry nodded grimly. Yeager wanted to talk, to raise hell with him likely, demand to know why he had failed to prevent Rufe Brock's death, and just what he was doing about the situation.

Glancing up and down the street and seeing no change, he started across. If George Yeager wanted to bitch, he'd listen — and if the man wanted his goddam job back, he could sure as hell have it. . . . Maybe this wasn't his last chance; maybe he could find another town somewhere that would offer him hope for the future.

"Hear Code's dead, too," the merchant said in a hard, accusing voice as the lawman came through the entrance. "You keeping it from me?"

Wade Henry halted in the center of the sprawling room. There was no one else present but the merchant and Old Amos, who was puttering around in the back.

"No —"

"The hell you wasn't! Wouldn't have known about it yet if one of that bunch you had lug Brock over to Schmitt's hadn't mentioned it."

"Was on my way to tell you when John Penny started yelling for me. No reason to hide it from you — rest of the town, yes."

Yeager rubbed his palms together and nodded, apparently satisfied. "You still ain't got no idea who's doing it," he said in a falling voice.

"Nothing good enough to work on."

The merchant cocked his head to one side. "What's that mean? If you've got a hunch about somebody, for Christ's sake lock him up! Who is it?"

"Forbes. Was out of town when Code was shot, and he had the time and opportunity to kill Brock."

Yeager stared at Wade. "Carson Forbes! Hell, man, that's crazy! Wouldn't be him."

The lawman's shoulders stirred. "You asked me if I had any idea — and that's it. Never said I had anything sure."

George Yeager swore again, mopped at his glistening face. "You can forget him. He ain't the one. It's somebody else and I'm having a hard time understanding why you can't get him pegged. My God, I can't go the rest of the day like this, sweating it out. Nobody else in town can either. We'll all be ready for the looney bin if you don't do something."

"Was thinking about that earlier. I won't quit you, but if there's somebody else around you want to take over, it'll be all right with me."

"Never said that —"

"Know you didn't, but it's plain you figure I ought to be doing better. Truth is, I've told myself that, but I can't think of anything to do that I'm not already doing."

The storekeeper took a cigar from a box in a nearby glass case and thrust it between his lips. Having a second thought, he picked up the cedar container and offered it to Henry, who refused with a wave of his hand. Yeager returned the box to the case and bit off the end of the weed. Striking a match, he puffed it into life agitatedly.

"Forget it," he said. "But I can't help being worked up plenty over this thing. Ain't thinking about putting somebody else on the job — not even if I had another man around willing to take over. You just keep on doing all you can."

Wade Henry nodded. "Pleases me to hear you say that, but you've got the right to make a change — seeing as how so far I haven't done any good."

"Some," Yeager said "There's still four of us alive, and half the day's gone. For a man working against something he can't see, I'd say you was doing pretty fair."

The lawman's brows lifted in surprise. Yeager was changing his attitude fast — possibly because he had little choice.

"Not much I've done except keep a sharp

watch and try to make you all stay under cover. If you'll all do that I figure we'll finally force the killer into the open,"

"Good a plan as any. If Code had listened to you I expect he'd be alive now. Don't know about Brock."

"Was in bad shape when I talked to him early. Liquored up and not thinking straight, warned him to lock his back door — I couldn't find the key — but I guess he never got around to it. Was how the killer got to him."

"Then he adds up same as Jess Code."

"About the size of it. Just hoping you and Drum and Hugo Kline will use your heads and stay put — not take any chances. Got Taft holed up in my office with orders to stay there, so I don't have to worry about him none. Way things are this whole town's about to blow up in my face, but if everybody'll sit tight, I can work it out."

Yeager jerked the cigar from his mouth and bobbed his head. "You can bet on me staying put! I'm not about to show myself out there and collect a bullet."

"Glad to hear it," Henry said and swung about for the door. "Time I was moving on."

The storekeeper bobbed again, forcing a smile. "Good luck, Marshal."

"Reckon that ought to go for all of us," Henry replied, and returning to the sidewalk, resumed his slow, careful patrol.

Forbes was in his office looking over papers of some kind scattered about on his desk. There was no one in the adjacent Alamo Saloon, and a moment later when he had passed the building he saw the Texan again taking his ease under the tree in the back. Continuing, he crossed to the end building where Schmitt, Wayland, and the others conducted their businesses.

The physician's sign was gone from his door but he was not visible inside, and Henry moved on, checking with both the café and Simon concerning strangers. He learned nothing. Ramrod straight in the streaming sunlight, his spine prickling, he cut over to ask the same question of Arky and the bootmaker, Zakowski. Neither could offer any help so he pushed on, having his look once more in the empty print-shop building and halting finally at Kline's livery stable.

The stable owner was napping in a room at the rear of the building, he was told by the blacksmith who had closed down his shop in the building's far corner and was passing the time playing two-handed poker with the hostler. After brief conversation with the two men, Wade dropped back to the street.

It was getting on to noon but he took no comfort in that as had George Yeager. Perhaps only two men of the six threatened were dead so far, but it took only a fleeting instant to snuff out a life, and the killer had all of the afternoon in which to complete his plan.

He halted. The door of Miss Camille's had opened, and Willa Sutton had stepped into the open. She was looking directly at him, her features soft and rounded despite the glaring light, as she paused at her own door.

"Marshal," she said, her voice low and serious. "I know you're hard pressed, but I think you'd best come in out of the sun for a few minutes. I've some apple pie, and there's fresh coffee."

Wade moved up to her, feeling the stir within him as always when she was near. He shook his head. "Afraid there's no time —"

"You should make time. You haven't stopped since early this morning — and I know you're hungry."

The lawman scoured the street with his glance. There was no change — no one in sight, no one at the windows or standing in the doorways or in the heat-filled passageways.

A slow smile cracked his haggard face. "All right," he said, and held the door open for her to enter.

13

Willa led Wade Henry through the store area of the building into the living quarters in the rear. Smiling, she motioned him to a chair at a small table placed midway between a window and the back door, both of which were open.

"There's no breeze, but it's a little cooler there," she said, turning to the stove.

The heat in the kitchen was oppressive but Willa did not seem to notice as she went about the business of filling cups with coffee and slicing the pie she removed from the stove's warming oven into thick wedges.

"Burl," she called, glancing to the top of the steps that led to the workshop above. "The marshal's here."

Sutton's acknowledging answer came at once, followed by a heavy thud as something fell to the floor. Willa smiled again at the lawman, placing a saucer of pie and a cup of coffee before him.

"He's always knocking things off his workbench. He needs a larger shop. It's so crowded up there."

She looked again to the stairs as Sutton appeared and began to descend, wiping his hands on a rag as he came down. He nodded to Henry, his face somber.

"Terrible thing about Brock — and that rancher, Code," he said, seating himself at the table. "Having any luck running down the man who did it?"

Wade said, "No, not yet."

"Still hoping he'll show himself, that it?"

The lawman waited until Willa had taken her place. "About the size of it," he said then. "Figure if I can keep the others hid out, it'll force his hand."

The girl frowned. "Hid out? I thought I saw Mr. Yeager in his store —"

"Reckon you'd not really say hid out. Just mean they're staying inside, not getting out in the open where they'd be an easy target. . . . Pie is the best I ever tasted."

Willa Sutton lowered her eyes. "Thank you."

Burl toyed with his fork. "What happens if Yeager and the others make it through the day? You think that'll end it?"

"Guess it's up to the killer. Could be he'll give it up, move on. He made such a big deal about doing it all in one day — the anniversary day somebody called it — that if he fails he just might call it off."

"Sounds like you think he's crazy — a lunatic."

Henry paused in his eating. "Has to be. Setting out to murder a half a dozen men and burn a town to the ground because of something he doesn't seem to have any connection with is plenty crazy. Sane man would go to the law if he had a reason to want something done about the Dolan lynchings."

Sutton continued to play with his fork, impressing short lines on the tablecloth with the tines. He was no stranger to fresh pie and similar good cooking, and didn't appear overly impressed by it. One of the advantages of having a wife, a home, Wade thought.

"Can't agree with you," Burl said, finally. "A man bent on revenge don't have to be crazy. And I don't think he'll quit at sundown if he hasn't finished what he set out to do. He'll hang around until he does."

"Could be right. What I'm trying to do is make it hard for him, bring him out where I can get to him, before sundown."

"Expect you're right, it will force him," Sutton said, beginning to eat. He rolled his bite of pie about in his mouth, then nodded to his wife.

"This is the best you ever made, Willa. The marshal's right."

"There's more," she said, reaching for the pan.

The lawman raised his hand in protest. "No thanks. Had all I can manage — and I'd best be moving on."

Sutton dropped his fork onto his plate, pushing back the chair. "No need to hurry. Imagine walking the town the way you are gets pretty tiresome in that hot sun."

"No other answer," Henry said, rising. He inclined his head to the girl. "Obliged for the pie and coffee. Was a treat a single man seldom gets to enjoy."

"Your own fault," she replied crisply.

"And our door's always open to you, Marshal," Burl Sutton added.

Henry, hat in hand, crossed to the door in the back of the room. "Think I'll go out this way," he said. "Like to keep things mixed up a bit. Thanks again, Mrs. Sutton."

Willa nodded, a smile still parting her lips as she began to clear the table. Burl, taking up the rag he had used to wipe his hands, followed the lawman into the open.

"Didn't want to ask in front of the wife," he said in a low voice as Henry stepped off the landing, "but Brock — heard he was stabbed."

"Pitchfork —"

Sutton swore quietly. He frowned then, his

pale eyes narrowing. "Don't know whether it means anything or not, but I saw that land seller, Forbes, come in about a half hour or so before you found Brock. Not accusing him but —"

"I'm keeping tabs on him," Wade said.

"Figured maybe you were, and it'll be smart to watch him close, I'm thinking."

Henry said, "Aim to do that," and started on down the alley behind the buildings, caution again placing its restraint upon him. He had known a few pleasant minutes of relaxation under the Suttons' roof, but that brief, unguarded time was over, and the searing heat and breathless tension that stifled the cringing town now again faced him.

He scanned the area behind the buildings, probing the stacks of empty boxes and barrels on the one side, and the dusty, sun-shriveled brush on the other with his glance, but he saw nothing that warranted attention. Reversing himself, he doubled back to the vacated building on the yonder side of Kline's, and on a hunch, entered.

The hunch proved of no value. Returning this time to the street, he started his slow, painstaking walk along its dusty length, pointing for the jail at the opposite end. Andy Taft would be growing hungry. He'd best see what the old deputy would like and fetch it to him from the hotel restaurant.

Once again he trod the hushed distance, searching the doorways, the passageways between the buildings, noting the empty windows, and came finally to the structure housing his office and jail. Taft, shirt off in deference to the heat, sweat glinting on his sagging skin, met him at the entrance.

"Nothing?"

Henry tossed his hat onto the desk. "Nothing," he said bluntly. "Can't figure where he's holed up — and walking the street's a waste of time, seems."

"Doing some good," the deputy countered. "Else you would've spotted him. Seen you go into Yeager's. He raising plenty of hell?"

"Some. Surprised me a bit. Agreed I was doing all I could." The lawman paused as the rattling of a wagon and the thud of horses' hooves broke the quiet.

Stepping to the door, he looked out. A man with a sun-bonnetted woman on the seat beside him were wheeling into town and angling toward the general store.

"That's Bill Avery and his missus," Taft murmured. "Coming to buy something. Reckon they forgot about what day this is."

Henry watched the pair draw up to the rack at Yeager's, climb down stiffly from the wagon, and enter the store as the dust stirred up by their arrival settled back into place.

"We was talking about Yeager," the deputy said. "He say anything worth mentioning?"

"Not much," Wade replied, turning from the doorway. "Figures I'm all wrong about Forbes."

"Expect he would. I recollect hearing they got a deal cooking on some land Forbes aims to buy. He looks like a good bet to me. He still around?"

"In his office. I'm watching him, no matter what Yeager thinks. He rides out again, I'll be following him. Want to see if he goes somewhere or just makes it look that way, and then doubles back."

"Won't surprise me none if that's what he's doing. You eat?"

"Had a piece of pie and a cup of coffee with the Suttons."

"Suttons, eh? She sure is a mighty fine looking woman —"

The lawman bobbed his head in agreement. "He thinks Forbes needs watching, too. You want something to eat? I'll run over to the restaurant, get it for you."

"Am getting a mite gant. Maybe a couple of them roast beef sandwiches — and some beer. Go plenty good, hot as it is."

The rattle of a wagon again echoed along the empty street. Henry swung to look and saw the Averys curving away from Yeager's. As they passed, the homesteader was leaning forward and plying the whip to his team, evidently anxious to get far from the settlement as quickly as possible.

Andy Taft grinned, wiping the sweat from his face as the clatter began to fade. "Guess old Bill's remembering now what this day is! About them sandwiches and that mug of beer —"

The shrill, piercing scream of a woman split the hush. Henry pivoted, snatched up his hat, and raced the length of the jail to its rear door.

Pete Drum lay face down on the grass half way between the hotel and his home near the creek. A woman, his wife, Wade thought, followed by two men and a young boy, was running toward him, crying her fear with each step.

14

12:05 P.M.

A weary impatience slogged through Wade Henry. Drum, like Jess Code, had ignored his wishes. He had gambled and had lost. Likely his thought had been to dash home for a bite of lunch, believing there'd be no danger in exposing himself for only the few moments it would require for him to cross from the hotel to his residence.

But it was no time for speculation; the killer was nearby, and by moving fast he might be able to get a glimpse of him. Hurrying to Drum's side was not necessary; the hotelman was probably beyond all mortal aid, anyway, and if still alive the two hired hands, his wife, and son could get him into the house and send for Doc Wayland. The woman's screams had also attracted others; a dozen or more persons were coming from the passageway that lay between Sutton's and the butcher shop, heading for the open ground.

"You two!" he yelled, beckoning to the

nearest of the men in the group. "I can use your help."

The punchers slowed, staring at him curiously. "Come on, come on!" he called irritably. "Whoever shot Drum's somewhere along the street. If we hurry it up maybe we can spot him."

The riders crossed to him quickly. The stockier of the pair said, "Sure, Marshal. What d'you want us to do?"

"Split up. You take the other alley, your friend can work this one. I'll handle the street. You see anybody with a gun or that looks like he might've just used one, throw down on him and yell. Understand?"

"You bet," the husky man said, and wheeled to his partner. "Let's go, Lafe."

Wade threw his glance at the cluster surrounding Pete Drum. He could see Wayland bending over the hotel owner, getting him ready to move. Whirling, the lawman started back for the jail at a trot, brushing by Taft standing just outside the door. The old deputy's face was angry.

"Pete — goddam him, he's killed Pete —"

"Maybe we've got a chance to do something about it this time," Henry said as he cut through the jail. "Killer's bound to be somewhere along the street."

Rushing on, he gained the front of the structure, then turned left. A few people were in sight, standing close to their doorways as if reluctant to stray far from protective cover. Throwing caution aside, Henry moved to the center of the dusty strip, and grim set, began a hurried journey to its opposite end.

The two men he had recruited to help were ahead, he knew, but since they were in the alleys behind the twin rows of buildings they were not visible to him. With luck, one would flush the killer from his hiding place and compel him to drop back to the street as he sought escape.

Raising his hand, the lawman waved the people along the walks into their buildings. It would be better if no one else was in sight; not only would it make it easier for him to notice someone emerging from one of the passageways, it also lessened the danger of an accident.

The walks cleared immediately, the Suttons and Miss Camille being the last to disappear, and he was again alone in the heated canyon between the buildings. He pressed on steadily, continuously sweeping the sides with his glance, not failing to include the building fronts, both lower and upper levels, in his search.

Abreast Yeager's he heard the merchant's hoarse voice reach out to him.

"Drum dead?"

Wade shifted his attention to the right. Yeager was a crouched shape inside his doorway.

"Looks that way," he answered.

Carson Forbes was standing close to the window of his office as he crossed in front of it. Henry gave the land broker a narrow look, wondered how long he had been there, and weighed the possibility of his being able to fire a bullet from some position on the opposite side of the street and return to his quarters without being noticed.

It could be done, he realized. The distance from the rear of Sutton's or Miss Camille's, or even the Enterprise Hotel, to Forbes' front door was less than a hundred feet. The man could have triggered a shot and made it back to his office easily before people along the street, attracted by the screaming of Pete Drum's wife, could have put in their appearance.

But there had been no sound of a gunshot. He and Andy Taft certainly would have heard it, had there been. Henry puzzled over that discrepancy as he pressed warily on in the tense heat. He thought back, reviewing the moments one by one as he sought the explanation.

Avery — and his wagon. The homesteader had been passing down the street at about that time, lashing his team into a run in his haste

120

to leave town. The old, well-used vehicle had set up a loud clatter, and it had been only a short time afterward that they had heard Drum's wife screaming.

That could be the answer. Still, there would have been a report, at least a faint one not entirely deadened by the noisy wagon, it seemed to him. It was hardly possible that the crack of a rifle or pistol had been submerged completely in the departure of the Averys.

Taut, the lawman moved on. The end of the street was not far ahead — the point where, very possibly, he would see the killer. With a man in each of the adjacent alleys and himself in the street, all moving forward, they could be driving the man before them, pushing him into the open.

Henry slowed. A coldness came over him, filling him with a strong warning. He took a quick half step to the side, spun, pistol leaping into his hand. An oath ripped from his lips as anger filled him. Andy Taft, arms cradling a rifle, was fifty yards behind him in the street. The old deputy was covering him.

"Get back!" Wade shouted, motioning.

Taft shook his head as the words echoed along the deserted hollow between the buildings.

"Never you mind," he answered.

Henry glared at the man. He was asking for a bullet — and he knew it. Why the hell couldn't he do what he was told? So be it. . . . It was neither the time nor the place to do any arguing. Coming around, he resumed his slow march.

Farther on, and to his left, he saw one of the punchers step out from beyond the far corner of Arky's saloon and take up a position. His partner would soon appear on the opposite side, near Simon's. Wade shrugged wearily. His plan had been a failure.

The rider who had patrolled the east alley came into view at that moment. He hesitated briefly at the side of the clothing store, then moved on to join his friend. Together they came forward to meet the lawman. The husky one, sweating freely, wiped at his face with a red bandana.

"Never seen nobody, Marshal. Looked sharp — and I even done some asking of folks that was standing at their doors. All claimed they didn't see nobody."

"Same here," Lafe added. "Don't think that jasper went down my alley."

Wade shook his head. "Reckon he gave us the slip again."

The squat puncher hawked, spat into the dust. A few strides away Andy Taft had halted, looking back up the street.

Lafe drew out his tobacco and papers and began to twirl a cigarette. "Was you asking me, I'd say that bird was holed up inside somewheres. That's why we didn't have no luck chasing him out."

Henry gave it some thought, then said, "Maybe. Seems somebody would've heard the shot. Did you?"

"Nope. We was in the saloon."

"Which one?"

"At the hotel — the Enterprise, I reckon they call it. All me and Shorty heard was that gal a yelling."

The lawman thanked the pair, turned, and started back up the street. There was some merit in the puncher's belief that the killer was hiding in one of the town's buildings, but logic was all against it. He'd not be in any of those occupied by their owners — they most certainly would have heard the gunshot even if they had somehow failed to notice the man.

The hotel — it was the only possibility. It was devoid of tenants, Drum had told him earlier, but the killer could have slipped in and stationed himself at a window of one of the second floor rear rooms. He would have then had an easy shot at Pete Drum as he struck out across the open ground that separated the structure from the hotelman's home. It was too late to hash it over now, but he guessed he should have thought to look through the upper floor rooms of the Enterprise the moment he had seen Pete Drum was down.

Angry with himself, he glanced up to Andy Taft, waiting for him in the shade of a tree.

"What the hell you doing — showing yourself —"

The old deputy tugged at a tip of his mustache. "What am I doing? I'm a doing my job, that's what. Sure wasn't about to let you go damn fooling down the middle of this here street without watching your backside for you. You're just plain-out bucking for the graveyard."

"Not as much as you are."

"Maybe, but I figured it wasn't my turn yet. Didn't roust out nobody, I take it."

Wade's features reflected his despair. "Got away, somehow."

"Mighty funny," Taft murmured. "Just can't see how he's doing it. Code, sure — man could have been setting his horse, pulled the trigger, and rode off before anybody knowed what was going on. But him a killing Brock and Pete Drum right here in town and nobody seeing or hearing a thing just don't make sense. . . . What's next?"

"Getting you off the street. Only you, Yeager, and Kline left. List's narrowing," Henry said, moving on.

Taft pulled a long step to one side and fell into pace. "Still thinking it'd be smart to sort of set me up like a tethered goat, for bait."

"Answer's still no to that," Wade snapped. "We get back to the office, you're staying there. If I want help from you, I'll yell for it, otherwise you keep under cover."

The deputy made no comment, and the two continued until they reached the building housing the jail. Once inside, Wade did not stop. Walking on down the narrow hall that fronted the cell block to the rear door, he halted there, throwing his glance to Drum's house. The sight of a short dozen persons gathered in the yard brought a frown to his forehead. Evidently Pete Drum had not been killed outright — and if still alive there was a chance he could shed some light on the identity of the killer.

Wheeling, he gave Taft a meaningful, warning look, and then stepping through the doorway, hurried across the burned-grass lot to the hotelman's home. Dollarhide, the barber, pushed forward from the crowd as he came up, his small, round face clouded with concern.

"You catch him, Marshal?"

"No luck," Henry said, and pushing on by,

mounted the steps to the verandah and entered the house.

He could hear low voices coming from a room at the end of a hall to his left, and made his way to it. Halting in the entrance, he saw Drum lying face down on a bed, a bandage striping his broad back. Nearby, Doc Wayland was replacing items he had removed from his bag. The hotelman's wife, son, and two women — probably close friends — were ranged against a wall.

The physician looked up as Wade stepped into the room. "Not dead," he said in his flat, to the point manner. "Got the bullet out, and he's resting easier. It'll be touch and go for a while."

Drum stirred sleepily and muttered, "Who is it?"

"The marshal," Wayland replied.

Henry crossed to the side of the bed, crouching to face the man. "Sorry about this, Pete —"

"No need — not your fault," Drum said thickly. "Was my doings. Ought've remembered, done what you told me to."

Henry had to lean close to catch the words. Behind him Wayland snapped his bag shut.

"Gave him some laudanum. He's about asleep."

Wade Henry nodded. "Pete," he said in a

strong voice. "Got to know. Did you see where the shot came from?"

Drum stirred again. "No. . . . Was just walking across the lot. . . . Hit me from . . . behind. . . . Never seen nothing. . . . Never heard nothing, either."

The lawman sighed, straightened up, and stepped away from the bed, aware of the women's frowning disapproval. He put his attention on Wayland.

"Anything you can tell me that'll help?"

The medical man set his bag on the chair beside him. "From what you said, I take it the one who did it got away."

Henry nodded.

"Can tell you this, the bullet went in just below the right shoulder. Judging from the angle it entered the body, it would have been fired from a height — and probably came from about the middle of town. That's assuming that Pete's back was turned square to the street, of course."

"Likely was," Henry said, forming a mental picture of the open field. "You think the shot could have been fired from an upstairs room in the hotel?"

"Be a good bet — particularly one of those at the upper end."

Wade again cursed himself for not looking into that possibility immediately after the shooting had occurred. But perhaps all wasn't lost; the clerk or a patron in the lobby or the saloon might have noticed someone loitering about. Asking a few questions in the Enterprise could prove to be a big help.

He wheeled for the door, paused, and faced the physician. "One thing — it'll be smart to let folks think Pete's dead, or at least that he's in a bad way and won't make it. Be safer for him."

Wayland said, "Understand what you're thinking. I'll take care of it."

Wade retraced his steps through the house and returned to the porch. As he started down the steps Dollarhide again broke away from the cluster of silent people gathered in the yard. The resigned passiveness he had seen in the inhabitants of Coyote Springs, those not on the killer's list, was gone now; genuine fear had taken its place. The town as a whole was sliding toward utter panic as the promised murders proceeded systematically on a deadly schedule.

"Marshal, is he —"

"Wayland'll be out in a minute," Wade said, hurrying on. "He'll give you the lowdown."

15

"Pete dead?"

Taft's question hit him as he entered the jail and walked to the front. He shook his head.

"Not yet. Wayland says it'll be close."

"He able to talk?"

"Some. No help, though. Didn't see where the shot came from. I'm heading over to the hotel, have a look upstairs."

The deputy scrubbed at his jaw. "You think the killer's holed up there?"

"About past the point of trying to think, but there's a chance he was."

Taft's thin shoulders twitched. "Well, he sure won't be there now," he said, unnecessarily.

The lawman, nerves honed to razor sharpness, brushed angrily at the sweat on his face. "Don't expect him to be," he snapped, and stepped out into the street.

Bitter, hard-set, Henry scoured the empty ribbon of dust with his gaze and stalked to the Enterprise. Mounting the broad gallery,

129

he entered and crossed to the desk. No clerk was present. He rapped the call bell impatiently.

The balding, elderly man employed by Drum in various capacities appeared at once in the archway that led into the saloon. He nodded, pushed his steel-rimmed spectacles higher on the bridge of his nose, and hurried up.

"How's Pete?" he asked, his features solemn.

"Bad. Could be he won't make it. Upstairs — the rooms across the back — anybody in them?"

The older man hesitated, glancing at the dozen or so keys hanging on a board behind the desk. "No, ain't nobody registered."

"Doors unlocked?"

"Yes, sure are. Always leave them that way till they're rented."

Henry pivoted on a heel and started for the stairway. The clerk followed anxiously.

"Why, Marshal? There something —"

"Want to have a look inside them." Wade paused, one foot on the lowest step. "You taking care of the desk this morning?"

"No, Pete was looking after things. I was busy —"

"Then you wouldn't know if somebody came in, went up there?"

"Sure wouldn't, but I don't think there was. Key'd be took if he'd rented one."

"Not talking about renting. Like to know if there was anybody hanging around, or came in, and went upstairs."

The clerk thought for a moment, then wagged his head. "Not that I seen. Pete — he could tell you —"

"Drum's in no shape to tell much about anything. You ask around, see if you can find out. Maybe the bartender or one of the loafers saw a man going up."

"Yes, sir, sure will," the clerk said, and turned back for the archway.

Wade climbed the steps and passed down a short hall that intersected another at right angles. The wall lamp was not lit but he could make out four doors on its west side. Stepping up to the first, he grasped the china knob and threw it open.

A blast of stale, hot air struck him head on. Hand on the butt of his pistol, he walked in, giving the small, sparsely furnished cubicle a quick, searching glance as he crossed to the lone window in the center of the wall.

Raising the sun-faded blind, he peered out. The empty stretch of ground between the hotel and Pete Drum's house lay below in unobstructed view. It would have been easy to pick off the hotelman from that position as he crossed the small flat.

Wade drew back, attention on the sash lock that secured the window. Undisturbed dust covered the circular thumb rest; the frame had not been opened for days. . . . But there were three other rooms, and three more windows.

Wheeling, he returned to the hall, made his check of the succeeding, almost identical quarters. In each he found the sash locks in like condition — well covered with a film of yellow dust that was certain evidence they had not been touched for some time.

Thoughtful, he stood at the streaky glass pane of the last, and ignoring the blast-furnace temperature in the room, stared out over the broiling land. If the killer had not used one of the hotel's back rooms for his ambush, then where?

Angling his glance, he looked along the line of buildings standing on that same side of the street. Other than Sutton's, the Enterprise was the only two-story structure — and there was no back window in the gunsmith's upstairs work shop, only openings in the front and on the north and south walls.

Opposite the hotel, not visible to him, was the building in which Yeager had his store, and it, too, had an upper level. It was used for storage, he recalled, and the window was blocked. The same applied to Brock's feed store, which had a loftlike arrangement. Even if the openings on the second floor of those two structures had been accessible, leveling a shot at Pete Drum would have been an impossibility, Henry realized, because of the intervening bulk of the hotel.

Dejected and puzzled, Wade Henry turned for the door. He was wrong again; the bullet couldn't have come from higher than ground level. Undoubtedly it had been fired by someone standing in the mouth of one of the passageways opening into the alley. It had merely caught Pete Drum at an angle.

He returned to the lobby, his face dark in study. In the back of his mind something had stirred, was beginning to nag at his consciousness — a something that should be clear to him but would not come forth and make itself definite. If he —

"Marshal —"

The clerk's voice halted him, brought him back to the moment. He swung his eyes to the man, "Yeh?"

"Done some asking around, like you told me. Nobody seen —"

"Forget it — doesn't matter," Wade said. "Could tell by the dust the rooms haven't been used for quite a spell. Obliged to you just the same."

The older man said, "Sure, Marshal, any

time," and stepped aside as the lawman moved on into the archway where he could look into the saloon.

Four men were at one of the tables playing a desultory game of poker. Hanging over them were the garishly dressed girls he had seen earlier in the day.

"Something for you?"

Wade came about to face the bartender, nodded, and stepped up to the bar. "Little warm for whiskey, but I can use a shot."

"Expect you can," the aproned man said sympathetically, and poured out a measure of liquor and placed it in front of the lawman.

Henry took the small glass between a thumb and forefinger and began to twirl it slowly. "That card game been going on long?"

The bartender touched the players with his glance. "Started about the middle of the morning. They had rooms upstairs. Come down, ate, and been setting there ever since."

"Don't remember seeing them in town before."

"Nope, reckon you haven't. Passing through, one said. Joining up with a bunch that's heading down Mexico way for some reason."

Wade tossed off his drink. "They been outside?"

"Once. Got up and looked out the window

when that fellow was yelling for you in the street — was when Brock got killed."

"What about when Drum was shot?"

"Never stirred a bone. From the looks of them, a killing ain't nothing special. . . . Guess I'll be looking for a job. Dollarhide was by here a bit ago, said Pete was same as dead. Sure too bad. Was a fine fellow to work for."

Henry continued to toy with his whiskey glass. "You've been around here a long time. What do you think about all this?"

"The killings — that what you mean?"

The lawman nodded.

"Well, sure is somebody mighty smart, else he'd a been caught before now."

"That's what I'm finding hard to figure — how he stays out of sight."

"So's everybody else. Folks've been sort of scared right along, but now they're downright spooked."

"No danger to them, only the ones on that list."

"That ain't it now; it's him saying he was going to burn down the town. At first they wasn't worrying much about it. Guess they figured you'd have caught whoever it was before it got that far. But way it stands now, three men dead and that bird still running loose, they're getting plenty jumpy."

The barman hesitated, mopped at the

counter for a moment. "Meaning no disrespect, Marshal, but they're wondering if you're going to be able to stop him."

The lawman stirred wearily. "Got to admit I'm not doing much good so far."

"Ain't you got no idea a'tall who's doing it?"

"Nothing for sure yet," Wade said, purposely not mentioning his thin suspicion of Carson Forbes. At the fever pitch to which the town was rapidly mounting, a name mentioned could lead to trouble — possibly another lynching.

The bartender continued his scrubbing. "Well, sure hope you turn up something before dark — else this town's going to bust wide open."

Wade pulled back, dropped a coin on the counter, and swung toward the archway. He hadn't thought of darkness as a deadline that the killer could be keeping in mind but it was a possibility; dispose of the men on the list by that time, then fire the town. That could be the plan.

Entering the lobby, Henry turned for the door, pausing as a thought came into his mind. Glancing to the clerk, now behind the desk, he said: "Any of the front rooms empty?"

The man adjusted his spectacles. "Reckon they all are, Marshal. Was some fellows rented a couple but they pulled out this morning — that's them in the saloon playing cards now. You needing a room?"

Henry wheeled, headed back for the stairs. "Just want to use one for a bit — do some looking and thinking. If there's any charge I'll pay."

"Won't be none for that. . . . They're all unlocked. Just help yourself."

That one of the front windows would afford him a good view of the street and the buildings lining it, just as the rear openings had enabled him to look over the area behind the hotel, had occurred suddenly to Wade Henry. He might spot something that would lead to an idea — and he was desperate enough to try anything —

The crash of shattering glass broke the hush that claimed the town. The lawman froze, and then as fear clawed at his throat, he spun, plunged down the stairs, and raced across the lobby for the doorway.

If the sound meant what he thought it did, the killer had scored again.

16

Wade Henry reached the hotel's wide porch, and pulled up short. It was Yeager's. The large glass window that fronted the store was now a gaping, jagged-edged hole.

He caught a glimpse of Andy Taft to his right, standing in the doorway of the jail. Across the way Dollarhide, the barber, and a man in stained, baggy overalls and ragged straw hat were coming out onto the sidewalk. Farther down he could see others making an appearance, some of whom were edging slowly, cautiously toward the source of the falling glass.

"Watch the street!" he yelled to the deputy, and whirling, circled the hotel at a hard run.

The shot most likely came from the side opposite Yeager's building. If he moved fast enough there was a good chance he could catch a glimpse of the killer hurrying as he sought to make an escape.

He turned into the alley, pistol in hand, then

halted. There was no one to be seen. The lawman swore savagely and continued on, crossing behind the hotel and the shops adjoining it — Sutton's, Miss Camille's — and came to Kline's.

The hostler and the young boy were standing at the corner of the wagonyard looking down the street. Both turned to face him as he stepped into the open.

"You see anybody come by here?" he called from the edge of the vacant lot.

The hostler shook his head. "Ain't nobody been this way. . . . It Yeager?"

"Don't know yet," Wade replied, and wiping at the sweat misting his eyes, resumed his steady tread.

He gained the rear of the livery stable, crossed its width, and now, more cautious, approached the vacant building beyond it. He was not doubting the hostler's words, it was simply that he had to be dead sure — and the stablehand could have been looking the other way.

He reached the one-time print shop quietly, spent a few moments with an ear to the dry, wood wall listening. The only sound was the clacking of insects. Stepping to the door, he pushed it open and entered.

The heat inside was monstrous. Ignoring it, he gave the place a swift going through, found no sign that anyone other than Texas Jack Kincaid had been there, and cut back to the alley.

He pushed on, checking with Zakowski and Arky, both of whom told him they had seen no one pass the way. Baffled, Wade Henry returned to the street. It was inconceivable the killer could disappear so quickly — and so completely — but he had.

Halting at the corner of Kline's barn, he looked toward Yeager's. A half a dozen townspeople, overcoming their apprehension, were gathered on the porch. He could see shadowy movements beyond the broken glass window, and guessed Doc Wayland and a few others were inside.

Drenched with sweat, he shifted his gaze to the open ground behind the row of buildings along which he had just traveled. Considerable space separated the structures from the grove where residences had been built.

A man might be able to fire a rifle from that point, aiming through one of the passageways that lay between the buildings, and reach his target. But the distance from the trees would be too far for accuracy, and if the marksman made the attempt from the proper range, somewhere near the middle of the flat, he would certainly have been noticed. . . .

And, too, the report of his rifle would have been heard.

Shaking his head, Wade Henry moved on, walking down the center of the street as he pointed for Yeager's. He glanced neither right nor left, avoiding the eyes of persons standing along the way but nevertheless feeling the quiet accusation in their looks. He had failed them — had failed himself, but the blame they reproached him with was no greater than that which he felt personally.

He came to Yeager's, mounted the steps to the porch, and pushing through the silent crowd, entered the building. Wayland was standing before an elderly woman who was seated on a chair. The physician, a small vial of ammonia in his hand, was watching the woman intently as she sobbed uncontrollably into a handkerchief.

Beyond them the body of George Yeager, covered by a new blanket evidently taken from stock, lay on a counter where bolts of dry goods ordinarily were stacked. Hovering close by, a glazed stare in his eyes, was Old Amos.

Dollarhide, and Cook from the Alamo Saloon, pulled away from the onlookers gathered inside the store and drew near Henry. The barber's voice was low, almost a whisper. His features were grim.

"One more dead, Marshal."

"Don't have to be told that," Henry said in a ragged tone.

He swung his attention to the shattered window. From it most of the street was visible. The bullet could have come from any point except those structures immediately adjacent to either side — Forbes' office and the barbershop.

He could guess what had happened. Yeager, ignoring or momentarily forgetting his warning, had stepped up close to the broad sheet of glass. The killer, patiently awaiting just such an opportunity, had triggered his weapon with deadly accuracy. But that assumed knowledge was of little help. He turned to the barber.

"She the only one with George when it happened?" he asked, motioning at the elderly woman.

"Her and Old Amos," Dollarhide replied. "He was filling her order, she said. Went up front to get something. Next thing she heard the glass bust. Said she thought somebody'd throwed a rock through it, then she seen Yeager falling with blood coming from his chest. Amos was in the back."

Henry gave the barber's words thought. "Your place is right next door — didn't you hear the shot?"

Dollarhide wagged his head. "Never heard

nothing, 'cepting that glass busting and coming down."

"See anybody on the street?"

Again the man shook his head. "Wasn't a soul, I'll swear to it — and I come out the second I heard the window bust."

Schmitt, accompanied by two helpers, came in through the back entrance at that moment. They stepped up beside the counter where the storekeeper lay, spread a stretcher on the floor, and placed the covered body upon it. As his assistants moved to go, the undertaker paused.

"Has his missus been notified?" he asked of no one in particular.

Wayland nodded. Schmitt bowed slightly and quietly followed the pair with the stretcher out of the store.

"Leaves only Kline and your deputy," Cook said as the door closed behind the small procession. "Marshal, you're needing some help."

"Got just about everybody in town doing what they can now — watching. No need for them to take up guns. That's my job."

"Problem's to spot whoever it is," Dollarhide added.

"That's it — and so far I've had no luck. I'll say it again, I'm open to advice."

Cook shrugged. "Not being a lawman, I ain't much on running down killers, but seems there ought to be a way."

Henry looked through the gaping window into the burning street. Small pinwheels of dust were whirling in the slight draft created by the passageway between Miss Camille's and Sutton's building. He raised his glance to the level of the gunshop. Willa and Burl were behind the display case — Miss Camille, he thought it was on the other side, or it could have been a customer. He wondered what Willa's opinion of him was at that moment, guessing that her estimation of him had dropped considerably, as it unquestionably had with others in the settlement.

There was no substitute for success, he realized as a slim thread of bitterness ran through him. A man could do his best even in an admittedly impossible situation, and if he failed, there was no remission.

No allowance would be made for the fact that Yeager and the three others had made it easy for the killer to strike by their own carelessness and bull-headedness — that each had consciously or accidentally ignored his warning to stay under cover and not expose himself. This was canceled out by the fact that the assassin had scored and that he had been powerless to prevent it — and that was synonymous with failure.

"Maybe it'd be smart for you to put Kline

and Andy Taft in a cell, lock them up, and keep them there until all this blows over," Dollarhide suggested.

"Might work — if it will blow over. Don't think that bushwhacker will quit until he's done what he came here to do. And I couldn't keep them locked up forever."

"No, suppose not, but I expect it'd sort of let folks simmer down for a spell and —"

Wade Henry wasn't listening. His glance, continually raking the street, had settled on Taft, still in the doorway of the jail. The old deputy was beckoning frantically to him.

17

"That Forbes jasper, he's riding out," Taft said as Wade, sweating freely from a hurried pace, halted in front of the jail. "Looks like he was just a waiting till everybody was sort of busy like and then rode off."

Henry followed the deputy's pointing finger with his eyes. The land broker was a small, mounted figure moving to the south. "Saw him standing in his office only a few minutes ago."

"Kind of funny, him pulling out right now. Yeager dead?"

Wade nodded, gaze still on Carson Forbes. The remoteness with which the land broker viewed the disaster threatening the town and the manner in which he held himself apart from it was strange; yet he professed to be interested in the area and its development. It would seem that a man with such in mind would be more concerned with its welfare.

"Think I'll just keep an eye on our friend for a bit," the lawman said. "Could be a waste of time — and maybe it won't be." He paused, faced Taft. "Can I depend on you staying inside?"

"I'm aiming to. What about Kline?"

"Not worried about him. He's the only one that's done what I told him," Henry replied, and entering the jail, made his way through it to the back where his horse waited under the sycamore.

"Not figuring to be gone long," he said, swinging to the saddle. "Don't you leave the place."

Taft, leaning against the door frame, bobbed his head. "Ain't stirring a inch — not now."

Henry pulled out from beneath the tree's spreading branches and headed into a sloping draw that angled toward the road. He supposed it didn't matter, but he would as soon no one saw him riding off; it apparently made little difference to the killer — assuming Forbes was not guilty — whether he was nearby or not.

Once well beyond the settlement, the lawman roweled the chestnut into a steady lope, now moving in a deep swale that not only placed him parallel with Forbes but kept him below the level of the land over which the man was passing.

As he rocked along to the motion of the horse his thoughts centered on the land broker. Many things pointed accusingly at the man, but all were merely circumstantial and had no sound basis in fact. He wished he did have something strong to go on; he then would feel inclined to jail Forbes, risk his outrage for the sake of those involved.

But his sense of fairness told him that would be the wrong course to follow — a belief now strengthened by George Yeager's death. For one thing, Taft had said the land buyer had a deal on to buy property from the merchant; he would hardly murder a man with whom he was about to transact business — if there was anything to his being in the profession to start with.

The lawman shifted on his saddle, loosening his shirt as he mulled that about in his mind. It could be just a front, a reason by which Carson Forbes was explaining his presence in Coyote Springs; but, on the other hand, he was unable to see how the man could have fired the bullet that killed Yeager and be able to return to his quarters unseen.

He, himself, had been on the street within only moments after the shot had cut down the storekeeper. The same applied not only to Andy Taft but to Dollarhide, the barber, and his overalled friend. None of them had seen Forbes or any one else cross from the side opposite the general store where the killer certainly would have had to be.

Wade's thoughts faltered. He frowned, brushed at the sweat beading his beard stubble as that deep-seated, gnawing disturbance buried in his mind again stirred, struggling to make itself known. He worked at it stubbornly, patiently, striving to bring it forth into clarity, but it seemed he could do no more than further confuse himself. It was there, however; something of importance, something that should be apparent to him. After a time he gave it up, cursing his inability to master his own faculties.

A quarter hour later he caught sight of Forbes through the shimmering layers of heat that lay upon the rolling countryside. The man had swung off the road and was slanting toward an area in the valley commonly known as the Tules. It was a small, marshlike section overgrown with cattails, black willow, and sawgrass, located in the center of a horseshoe bend in the river. The stream left its banks at that point to create a near swamp, then, farther down, rechanneled to regain its original course.

Veering the chestnut onto a more direct course, but maintaining his position below horizon, Henry pressed on. He could find little reason for Forbes to be looking over land in that section of the Palomas Valley. Because of the high alkali content of the soil it was considered of no use or value.

He pulled the gelding to a halt behind a clump of doveweed. Forbes had stopped, and from the summit of a knoll was studying the marsh. A pair of summer ducks, disturbed by his appearance, rose from the weeds, and lifting swiftly on pointed wings, bore south, following the river's course. Elsewhere in the rank growth, a dove called sadly.

The land broker dismounted, and tethering his horse to a bush, walked down into the sink and once again paused. Watching closely, the lawman saw him dig into the pocket of his corduroy breeches and produce a square of paper. He unfolded it slowly, apparently making some sort of comparison with the land itself. . . . A map, Wade concluded; Forbes was getting landmarks established in his mind.

The land broker continued to pore over the paper and then, finally satisfied, he returned it to his pocket and walked slowly back to his horse. Climbing onto the saddle, he swung the animal around and struck due east.

Wade Henry shrugged. There was little doubt now; Carson Forbes, despite all indications, was not the man he was looking for; he was, instead, just what he claimed to be — an investor bent on making a fortune in land.

Cutting the chestnut about, the lawman headed back for the settlement. Following Forbes had been a waste of time, just as had been the close watch he'd kept on him in town. But there had seemed good reasons for it then.

He was now left with no suspect.

The lawman swore softly at that realization. Every idea, every possibility he had managed to come up with had turned sour. He had to admit that he was at the end of his rope.

But he couldn't quit. Somehow he must run the killer to ground, stop him before he could take the lives of the remaining two men on the list and carry out the threat to burn the town. Three dead now — four if Pete Drum didn't pull through — and he'd been helpless to prevent it. As a lawman he was falling far short.

Jerking his bandana from a pocket, he wiped impatiently at the sweat on his face and neck. What the hell could he do? How could he flush the murderer from his hiding place? Maybe the answer was to form a sort of posse, get all the men he could persuade to help, and make a foot by foot, house to house search of the town by starting at the end of the street, and in forage-line formation, literally comb the settlement.

Or perhaps he should take Andy Taft up on his offer to act as bait, tempt the killer into making a move. It should work since there was only Hugo Kline and the old deputy left to be accounted for. Staking Taft out could be the solution — but it could also mean the death of Andy if things didn't go right, and so far they hadn't.

There had to be another way. He couldn't risk Taft's life, not if — the lawman's thoughts came to a halt. . . . Maybe putting out bait was the thing to do, after all! Not exactly along the lines the old deputy had in mind, but close to it.

A half grin cracked Henry's lips as he leaned forward on his saddle and urged the chestnut to a faster lope. By God, it just could be the killer hadn't beaten him after all!

18

By the time Wade Henry had pulled in under the tree behind the jail and dismounted, Taft was in the doorway awaiting him.

"Well?"

The lawman shook his head at the deputy. "Not the man we're looking for," he said, entering the building.

Tossing his hat onto the desk, Henry ran his fingers through hair plastered to his skull by sweat and crossed to the bucket in the corner of the room, treating himself to a drink. The water was warm but wet and it did relieve the crackle-dry coating in his throat.

"Anything happen while I was gone?"

"Nothing. Just gets hotter. If it ain't Forbes, then who —"

"Got an idea that maybe'll tell us," Henry said, moving to the window and staring off into the street.

"That's good," the deputy said, nodding. "Ain't meaning you ain't tried to wind this here thing up, but we sure better get something done. George getting his'n's about tore it for sure. What're you aiming to do now?"

"Use a little bait."

"Fine — I'm ready."

"Not you — Hugo Kline."

Andy Taft studied Henry with his watery eyes. "Huh? You think that's smart?"

"And safe," the lawman said. "Kline's got an office with a fair-sized window on the street-corner side of his building. I've seen him sitting there at his desk plenty of times."

"And setting there again right now he'll make it plumb easy for that killer to pick him off."

"What I hope — only it won't be Kline, just something that looks like him."

A slow grin spread across Taft's seamy, glistening face. "I savvy what you mean! You're figuring to use a dummy."

"That's it, and I'll be standing someplace that'll let me see where the shot comes from."

"It ought to work," Taft said in a satisfied voice. "Yes, sir, it sure ought to."

"It had better," Wade replied quietly, reaching for his hat. "Going over there now and set it up. When it's ready, I'll give you a high-sign. Want you to be watching, too — from here."

Stepping out into the street, the lawman

started the walk to the livery barn at the opposite end of the town. The heat was at its worst at that hour, but he had attained that point where body was numb to any increase in temperature, and sweat-soaked clothing had ceased to be a discomfort.

A tarp had been hung over the broken window at Yeager's and through the open doorway he could see Old Amos standing behind a counter. He noted a few faces peering at him from the depths of some of the stores, but when he drew abreast Sutton's and his glance shifted to the gunshop, he saw no sign of Willa.

He felt a small pang of disappointment at that. He would have liked taking a moment to pause, tell her that he perhaps now had the situation in hand and to worry no more; but she was not available and he couldn't very well go up to the door, knock, and call her out for that purpose.

The plan might fail, anyway, he realized. It could prove too obvious and the killer not fall for the ruse. He smiled grimly as he considered the possibility. So far luck had been against him at every hand; the odds that it would not change were better than good. He had to try, nevertheless.

He found Hugo Kline still in the rear of his establishment, passing the hot, dragging minutes by repairing a saddle. The remains of his lunch, evidently carried in by a member of his family, was on a nearby stool. The stableman had profited well by Pete Drum's experience.

"Have thee caught this madman?" he asked, looking up hopefully as Wade entered.

"Wish I could say yes, but he's still loose."

Kline sighed gustily and laid aside his awl. "A terrible day for this town."

"The worst. . . . Got an idea I'd like to work out with you."

The stableman nodded. "If I can help, Marshal —"

"You can," Wade said, and explained his plan. "Be a couple of minutes when it could be risky. That'll be when we go in your office and move about a bit, and you let yourself be seen. But I'll be with you and if the killer's watching I don't think he'll chance taking a shot."

"I am willing," Kline said in his slow, precise way. "When —"

"Now. Sooner we set it up, the better."

The older man got to his feet and together they walked the length of the runway and turned into the small, cluttered office. Henry stepped up close to the window at once, scanning the street while Kline seated himself at the dusty rolltop desk placed against the wall and began to rummage through the papers scattered upon it.

"Ought to do it," the lawman said after a minute or so had elapsed, and then as Kline rose and moved toward the door, he closed in behind him, effectively blocking the man off.

Again in the runway, the stable owner picked up a burlap bag from a pile in the corner, and crossing to the middle stall, held the sack open while Wade stuffed it with hay. That done, he removed his shirt, draped it about the sack, tying the arms across the front to maintain a semblance of shape, and then placed his familiar round black hat on the top. Dropping back he eyed the creation doubtfully.

"Does thee think it will fool anyone, Marshal?"

"From a distance," Wade replied, waiting while Kline pulled on a denim jacket as a replacement for the shirt he had been wearing. "Let's get it into your chair. I'll go in first, sort of hide you while you put it in place."

The lawman reentered the office, moving in front of the desk. Behind him Kline quickly placed the dummy on the hard-back chair, taking an extra moment or two while he got the distinctive headgear properly set before he returned to the runway.

Wade hung back for a bit, stirring restlessly about the small, heat-filled office, surreptitiously nudging the chair with his foot until he had the dummy worked into its most inviting position — back to the window — and then rejoined the stable owner.

"Next thing is for you to go back to your shop and stay there," he said, surveying the office through the doorway. "Looks pretty real, but I reckon that's not much of a compliment."

Kline was a humorless man. "It does not matter," he said. "The importance of it comes if it will trick the killer. . . . Is there word of Drum?"

"Still alive, last I heard."

"And George Yeager — it was quick I am told by the hostler."

"Expect he was dead when he hit the floor."

Kline shrugged tiredly. "It is so strange. A gun is used but it is heard by nobody. And thee can find no one in a town so small. I do not understand."

"We're in the same wagon there. I can't figure it either, but maybe this time we'll outsmart whoever it is. If not —" Wade let his words trail off.

"A sad day," Kline murmured, shaking his head. "Will thee wait here?"

"No. Don't think he's apt to make a try

with me hanging around close. I'm going up to one of the front rooms in the hotel. Can look down on the street and all the buildings on the other side from there. I'll be able to see anything that moves, but more than that, the smoke that'll come from a rifle when it's fired will show up plain."

"I see. A bullet will come from that side of the street, thee believes."

"Have to."

"But did not the one that killed George Yeager come from this side?"

"Way I see it, but there's no being dead sure."

"Then this killer, he would have to cross back —"

"Probably did after it was all over. Could've mixed in with the people that gathered around, not be noticed."

Kline frowned as he gave that consideration. "Then this madman is one of us — one of the town and not a stranger? Does thee believe that?"

"I'm beginning to," the lawman said. "One thing more, if he falls for the dummy trick, you still keep out of sight. Want him to think he's put a bullet in you whether I spot him or not."

"It is understood," Kline said solemnly.

Henry turned, walked the length of the stable, and broke out of its shadow into the street, making it evident that he was leaving. Swinging right, he headed for the Enterprise to carry out the next step in his scheme. His eyes fell upon the figure of Willa Sutton standing at the corner of Miss Camille's dress shop, and he slowed.

Her head was tipped down as if she were in deep thought, and Wade, a sudden shaft of brightness spreading through the somberness the day's events had laid upon him, grinned broadly and hurried up to her.

He halted before her, the smile drying up on his lips as he noted a darkness on one side of her face. "Is everything all right with you?" he asked, his eyes narrowing.

Willa did not lift her head, concealing the bruise from him. "Yes . . . I just came outside — for a breath of air."

The lawman moved up closer to the building into the strip of slowly forming shade alongside it. "Hot everywhere today," he murmured for a lack of anything better to say.

Her shoulders stirred listlessly. Henry continued to study her.

"You sure there's nothing wrong?"

"No, nothing more than usual," she said in a resigned voice. "I — I'm sorry we came here — ever left St. Louis."

"Was it better for you there?"

160

"In some ways. At least I had my relatives — and friends. Here I feel so alone . . . I realize more and more it was all a terrible mistake."

The lawman, hat in hand, brushed at the sweat on his face. "What was a mistake?"

Willa was silent for a long breath, and then she raised her head, looking at him squarely. The darkness along her cheekbone was a bruise, as he had guessed. Anger whipped through him but he said nothing; he would not humiliate her by obvious questions. He waited, seeing the faint glint of tears in her eyes, watched her lips form a word — one that died in a shake of her head as she thought better of it and left it unsaid.

"I'd like to know," he said gently. "Important to me."

Again she faced him, her skin aglow with a faint shine of moisture. "I've no right to burden you, of all people, with my troubles."

"Room for sharing yours — if it'll help."

"I guess there's nothing can do that. . . . It's just that things are not the same between Burl and me — not for the past year. I thought, in the beginning, that we'd always be happy, but it hasn't worked out that way."

"Never any guarantees in life," Wade said. "Is there anything I can do to help?"

"I don't think so, and perhaps it will change.

I — I keep telling myself that, only it never does — just gets worse."

He frowned, glanced to Kline's office, wishing he could get through to her, make her understand his deep interest. . . . The dummy looked real even at that close distance. . . . After a bit he brought his attention back to her.

"Maybe whatever it is that's bothering you isn't worth the fight. Sometimes it's that way — and you live but one time. Important you make the best deal you can before it's too late."

"But if you find it was all a mistake —"

"Then change it. That's the reason I'm here today, trying to do a good job for this town. Came to me that I was twenty-eight years old and had nothing to show for living that long. Decided my whole life was a mistake so far, and I'd best tie down, find myself before time ran out. Could be the same applies to you."

"How could I —"

"If you've come to realize you've picked the wrong man," he said, plunging into what he believed was the heart of her problem, "do something about it. Leave Burl. Lots of years ahead of you yet — be a fool thing to spend them in misery. And being happy comes natural and easy if you're with the right party."

She probed his dark, intent features with

candid, blue eyes. "Didn't you ever find the right party?"

Wade Henry shrugged. "Guess I never went looking. Was always too busy seeing what the next town looked like. If you want me to help — get you to a place where you can head back to St. Louis —"

"Could you do that?" she said quickly, a smile forming on her lips.

He was a long time in replying and there was a heaviness in his voice. "If that's what you want."

"I guess it is," she said, sighing. "Maybe I really don't know yet. I'd like to think about it."

"That's the thing to do," he said gruffly. "Be plenty sure and then make up your mind. My troubles will end here tonight, one way or the other. Tomorrow'll be a different day. If you want me to fix it up so's you can get out of here, just say the word."

Willa reached out impulsively, laid her hand on his arm. "Thank you, Wade," she murmured in a grateful voice.

"One thing more," he said, eyes touching the bruise on her face, "I can put a stop to that, too. You can move into the hotel and I'll warn him —"

Her fingers had gone to her cheek in a futile gesture of concealment. A glow of embarrassment suffused her skin.

"No . . . I'll be all right."

At first he had avoided mentioning the blow she had obviously received at the hands of Burl Sutton, wanting to spare her feelings. That had all changed.

"I won't stand for him treating you bad. I'll —"

"Please — just forget it. It was probably my fault. . . . And I don't want him hurt on my account."

The lawman shrugged. Understanding her was beyond him, but if that was the way she wanted it, so it would be.

"Whatever you say."

She managed a smile. "Thank you, again," she said, and wheeling, turned the corner and disappeared.

Henry stood motionless, the faint, womanly fragrance of her lingering in his nostrils, and then as he heard the screen door of the gunshop close, he drew on his hat and moved once more into the street.

19

Wade Henry paused long enough at the jail to alert Andy Taft to the fact that his plan for trapping the killer was in effect, and to keep a sharp lookout. Then he entered the hotel.

The clerk was nowhere to be seen in the strangely silent building, and he mounted the stairs and made his way to a room in front center of the upper floor without encountering anyone.

Taking care to attract no attention, he drew aside the curtains to a point where he could look down on the street and the structures opposite without difficulty. After that, keeping below the window's level, he raised the square of framed glass to its top and settled back as a rush of fresh, if hot, air flooded into the stale-smelling quarters.

Pulling out his bandana he wiped the sweat from his face and neck and scrubbed at his wet, flattened hair. He felt somewhat better then, and hitching up close to the window sill, he began a careful, methodic search along the buildings opposite.

As before, all appeared bleak and deserted under the lash of the sun. The gray fronts, the warped timbers and cracking boards betraying their age, would be quick fodder for the killer's torch, he thought, and a fire once started would be hard to check.

Hitching himself to one side, he managed to see the front of Kline's livery barn and was able to catch a view of the office. The hay-filled sack with its distinctive hat and gray shirt appeared lifelike as it filled the stableman's chair and hunched over the desk. The plan should work, but the way things had been going for him, he could only hope.

He brought his attention again to the street, resumed his patient probing, studying the mouth of each passageway opening into it, every window and door facing it, even the irregular line of overlooking roofs. There was no one visible along its entire east side.

He felt there was little cause to worry about the structures rising to either side of the hotel. There would be no danger of course from the jail, the only building to the right, and those succeeding to the left would not afford a shot at the target so carefully placed in Kline's office. A bullet would have to come from the opposite side — and any man lining up his rifle for an attempt must do so in view of the hotel window.

Wade grunted his satisfaction with the arrangement, and drawing his pistol, laid it on the sill. It might become necessary to act quickly when — and if — the killer revealed his presence. He would be ready.

The minutes wore on. Two punchers entered the street at its southern end and rode its full length to the Alamo Saloon. They picketed their horses at the side and entered. Then two elderly women, primly defying man and weather, came from the houses along the creek and walked boldly to Yeager's, where they climbed the steps to the porch and disappeared inside.

But there were no other indications of life in the breathless, hushed tension that strangled activity, and the presence of the passing riders and the elderly women seemed oddly out of place and far from the norm.

The lawman's mind drifted to Willa Sutton. He thought of how she had looked when he had met her, only minutes earlier, and went slowly over the words she had spoken to him. She had reached the end of her rope insofar as her life with Burl was concerned, that was plain. He wondered how much abuse she had taken from the man, and anger stirred him again as he visualized, in his inner eye, the dark evidence of that abuse. It was a hell of a thing to be happening to her but he could not blame her for wanting to bring it to an end.

She had not been certain, had seemed undecided, but he guessed he could understand her reluctance. To admit failure and defeat in a marriage was as difficult as facing up to it in anything else. And a woman would find it harder than a man since her marriage was essentially her life.

He would hate to see her leave. The few occasions when he had been with her had lifted him somehow, encouraged him to hope and perhaps reach for higher things. With her no longer around it would be as if a light had gone out somewhere bequeathing him only the ordinary in life.

He wondered if she had purposely waited for him while he was in Kline's, and to believe so pleased him. To have her turn to him for comfort, even if for so brief a time, touched him deeply. She would get his help; she needed only to ask, and regardless of personal cost, he would not fail her.

Henry leaned toward the window, scanning again the facades that stared unseeingly back at him through the sullen, hot silence of the street. It came to him suddenly that finding himself, his niche in the future, no longer mattered; what did count was that Willa find her place and the happiness she was entitled to.

The two women appeared in Yeager's doorway, paused for a short time to examine their surroundings, and then, packages tucked under arms, stepped down into the dust, crossed, and passed beyond his range of vision below.

He remembered then he had forgotten Taft's lunch. The old deputy would be plenty hungry by that hour — but he'd live through it, and that was more than could be said for Yeager and Brock and Jess Code, and perhaps Pete whose life still hung in the balance.

Andy would be remembering that and it would dull his need to some extent. He would be thinking, too, that his turn with the killer would be next after Hugo Kline was taken care of — possibly even before. Wade doubted that, however; the deputy would be the most difficult for the killer to reach, unless he forgot himself again and senselessly exposed himself on the street. But he had been lucky those times, and knew it. It wasn't likely he'd make the same mistake again, not with his name at the top of the list.

Wade leaned back, stretching his long length. The faded carpeting on the floor was worn and thin, and afforded little cushion between his body and the hard boards. He shifted again, drew himself to a squat, and bunched on his heels while his glance once more scoured the street.

A lone woman, apparently emboldened by the two previous shoppers, appeared. Apron folded back and tucked under its strings, sunbonnet shading her features, she made her way hurriedly into Yeager's. Returning almost immediately, a can of something in her hand — baking powder, Henry thought — she crossed the porch and hastened out of sight. Men had died, a whole town was threatened, but daily life must go on, regardless.

The lawman pivoted away from the window and rose to ease his aching muscles. Digging into his shirt pocket he produced the thick, nickeled watch he'd picked up once when he was in Abilene. . . . Ten until four. . . . He hadn't realized how long he'd been pegged at that window in the hotel room; the minutes had seemed to drag. Tucking the timepiece back into its place, he moved once more into position.

How much longer should he remain there? He had thought the killer would make his try for Hugo Kline before then. Could he have seen through the ruse, recognized it for the trick that it was? Could he have spotted the open window in the hotel, the parted curtains, and guessed that the town was under close surveillance?

Or was he simply biding his time, allowing the hot, withering moments to build the fear and tension he undoubtedly enjoyed inflicting upon the town and its people.

He'd give it until four-thirty, Wade decided, and if nothing had happened, he'd forget it, admit his plan had not worked — and tot up one more failure to his credit.

20

4:35 P.M.

Wade Henry flung his hat onto a chair and shrugged wearily. "Didn't work. He never fell for it."

Taft dropped his gaze, staring at the dusty floor of the marshal's office. "Outsmarts us no matter what we come up with."

The lawman made no reply. He was tired of trying; success would have no part of him — he was fate-branded to never attain accomplishment in anything.

"So I reckon that's that," the old deputy said, dropping onto one of the benches set against the wall. His features were beet red from the persistent heat that still showed no signs of breaking, although the day was growing late. He rubbed vigorously at the stubble on his chin.

"Well, there ain't no use mooning about it. What do you figure to do now?"

"What the hell can I do?" Henry snapped irritably. "Go out there in the street and watch

172

and wait — and listen to you or Kline die when my back's turned!"

"Ain't no man can do more'n you're doing," Taft said quietly. "If that killer gets me, want you to know that I was feeling that way and ain't blaming you for nothing — not one whit."

Wade glanced at the deputy. "Appreciate that, but it don't help much," he said, the sharpness gone from his voice. "My job's to keep you and Kline alive, same as it was for the others. . . . I'm not cutting the mustard."

"Town ain't big, but nobody could expect you to be in two places at the same time. Got me a feeling I should've been out there with you, helping. Much my fault as yours that Yeager and —"

"You'd be dead right now, too, if you'd tried," Henry cut in, crossing to the water bucket and helping himself to a drink.

"Maybe, but you sure should've had some help, like a couple of extra deputies to make the rounds."

"Nobody was willing to take the job — you know that, and I can't blame them. You ever see Forbes ride in?"

Taft bobbed his head. "Half hour or so ago. From the east. Had in mind you'd see him."

"Coming in from the back side of the buildings, I couldn't have." The lawman picked up his hat, wiping the sweat band with his fingers. "Getting late. I'd best get out there —"

The faint clatter of falling glass at the far end of the street brought Wade Henry up short. For a long moment he stood motionless, staring at Taft, and then as realization struck him, he spun to the door.

"Kline — the dummy!" he shouted, and leaping through the jail's entrance, started up the street at a run.

Dollarhide shouted something to him as he hurried by but he paid no attention to the barber, ignoring him and the dozen others who had magically appeared along the way.

He reached the corner of Miss Camille's and saw the shattered window of the stableman's office. The dummy, dislodged by the impact of the bullet, had slipped from its chair and lay partly on the floor.

The lawman swore bitterly as he turned into the runway of the livery barn. He had been wrong; the killer had risen to the bait — only he had not been there to spring the trap. . . . If he'd stalled out another fifteen minutes at his post in the hotel room — but there was nothing to be gained in thinking of that now.

Inside the murky depths of the stable he came to a stop. At the opposite end he could see Kline. Beside him were the hostler and the boy he employed at times to do odd jobs.

"Did thee get him, Marshal?" the stable owner called.

Wade shook his head. "Caught me not watching," he said, making his blunt admission of failure immediately. "Stay back where you are." He beckoned to the pair with Kline. "Give me a hand up here. Got to let that killer think he's scored."

The boy and the hostler came forward at once, and with them, Henry entered the office. He glanced through the jagged remains of the glass. A half a dozen persons had collected in the lot between the barn and Miss Camille's and were looking toward the office. He recognized Mondragon from the butcher shop, Burl Sutton, and Dollarhide among them. Willa was not present. Farther down the street he could see a second cluster forming.

"Got to make them all think this is Kline," he said, stepping to the front of the office where his figure would hinder the view of the outsiders. "The two of you pick up the dummy, handle it like it was a dead man — make it look real."

The hostler and the boy bent over the sack of hay, lifted it carefully. Henry wheeled to the window, motioned to Dollarhide, just breaking away from the small crowd and coming nearer for a better look.

"Go after Schmitt," he ordered. "Tell him to get over here with a stretcher."

The barber halted. "That mean Kline —"

"Get Schmitt — and tell those people to get off the street!"

Dollarhide's features were wooden. He turned away at once, pausing to relay the lawman's words to the knot of bystanders, and then trotted on toward the undertaker's building.

Henry remained for a bit studying the street, watching it slowly clear, and then returned to the runway where Kline's helpers were waiting beside the dummy. The stableman was still in the rear of the building.

"Marshal — I do not understand. The trap, it worked, but thee said —"

"I'd given it up," Wade replied. "Figured the killer had spotted the dummy for what it was and passed it by."

He hesitated. Kline's likeness had been in place for a considerable length of time — almost three hours, in fact, before the killer had chosen to put a bullet into it. Why had he delayed so long? That he would have fired his shot much earlier seemed more logical. Could it be that he was not in town during that time?

As that thought crossed his mind, Henry's suspicions reverted instantly to Carson

Forbes. He had ridden out shortly after Yeager's death, had returned only minutes before a bullet smashed into Kline's dummy. Was it coincidence?

"Marshal —"

Henry came about as Schmitt and the two men he had evidently hired for the day walked through the barn's wide entrance.

"Here's the body," he said, pointing.

Schmitt stared at the sack of hay. "I — I reckon I ain't getting what you mean," he mumbled. "Where's —"

"Kline's all right," Wade explained, jerking a thumb at the stableman waiting in the rear of the building. "Was that gunny sack full of hay the killer shot — but I want everybody to think it was Kline. Understand?"

Schmitt nodded. "Guess I do. You're telling me to handle this just like it was Hugo."

"That's it."

The mortician motioned to his associates. Opening the stretcher, they placed the dummy upon it, pulling some of the hay from its open end to attain length, and then draping a woolen blanket over all.

Schmitt stepped back, surveying the arrangement approvingly. "Looks real, I suppose, but I can't say I know for sure what —"

"There's only one man left on the list now — my deputy," the lawman said grimly. "I'll guarantee you that killer will have one hell of a time getting to him!"

Wade did not miss the fleeting expression of skepticism that crossed the undertaker's face. It brought a flash of anger to him, but he held his peace. He knew he could not blame Schmitt, or any of the townspeople for what they were thinking; he had accomplished nothing to warrant confidence.

Schmitt nodded to his helpers. Stooping, they took up the stretcher and moved toward the door. The undertaker fell in behind them and the slow procession entered the street, slanted for the funeral parlor.

Henry watched until they reached the building and disappeared inside, relieved that none of the townspeople felt called upon to intercept the party. Then he faced Kline.

"Stay hid. The killer finds out he's made a mistake, he'll try again."

The stableman murmured his agreement. Henry, thoughts still on Carson Forbes, whose building was almost directly opposite, said, "Where'd it sound like the shot came from?"

Hugo Kline's moon face pulled into a frown. "I hear no shot, Marshal. Only the window breaking." He shifted his attention to the hostler and the stableboy. The boy shook his head.

"We didn't hear no shooting, either."

"Where were you?" Wade asked, realizing that neither he nor Andy Taft had noticed a gunshot, just the shattering glass. That they were inside a building at the opposite end of town could possibly account for this, but a man near enough to the stable to fire into the dummy surely was heard by someone.

"Right there in that stall," the hostler said, pointing to the third compartment off the runway. It was only a few strides from the open doorway.

"Hard to believe," the lawman murmured. "Shot had to come from somewhere close."

"Well, that's sure'n hell the way it was," the hostler said, nettled. "I wouldn't be telling you no lie about it!"

Henry reached out, laid a hand on the man's shoulder. "Not doubting your word. Never heard any of the shots myself. Nobody else did. Just that I'm trying to figure how —"

"Fire!"

21

At the cry of alarm Wade Henry spun and raced into the street. Others were there ahead of him; still more were coming from their doorways.

"It's Brock's!" a voice shouted.

Black smoke was boiling up from the rear of the feed store. Tips of flame tongues were licking along the roof's edge.

The lawman broke into a hard run down the center of the dusty way. Men, carrying buckets and other containers that happened to be handy, were converging on the structure. Their faces were strained and Henry could read panic in their eyes. The killer had made good his promise; he had slain the men involved in the lynching of the Dolans, and was now completing the threat by putting a torch to the town.

He reached the feed store. The back wall was already a mass of seething flames. A bucket line had been formed at the horse trough behind Yeager's, and men were passing water forward as rapidly as they could. They were making little headway. The powder-dry wood of the structure was burning furiously despite their steady effort.

"Over here! Bring them buckets over here!"

It was Andy Taft's voice. Henry saw the deputy mobilizing the new volunteers into a second line of fire-fighters. He swore harshly. Taft had no business there in the open, inviting a bullet.

Dollarhide, face dripping sweat, clothing smoking in several places where sparks had fallen, appeared suddenly in the thickening haze. His arms were loaded with possessions that he was removing from his shop, which, being connected to Brock's, was unquestionably doomed.

"Was him!" the barber shouted as Wade turned to him.

"Who?" the lawman yelled back, making himself heard above the crackling flames. "Who did you see?"

Dollarhide dropped his belongings in the middle of the street, wheeling for a second load.

"Nobody — didn't see nobody . . . but I smelled coal oil just before I seen the fire. It's that killer doing just what he said he'd do!"

Henry hurried on, pointing for the rear of the burning building. The abandoned structure to its left was now beginning to smoke as falling embers settled upon its rotting timbers and found purchase. No one was bothering to halt the spreading flames there; keeping the fire from moving north to Yeager's and the succeeding buildings in the row was more important.

He reached the rear of Brock's, and swept the laboring, sweating men with his glance. Taft was at the water trough, dipping and passing buckets in a steady, rhythmic motion. The lawman crossed to him.

"Get back to the jail," he shouted. "I'll take over here."

The old deputy turned a soot-streaked face to him. "Reckon I'll be all right. You best keep looking."

"Goddammit — you're making a target of yourself!"

"Can't see as it matters none," Taft replied without pause. He swung his glance to the man at the pump. "Get working that handle faster, Ernie! We're a catching up to you!"

The vacant structure to the south was now a cradle of fire with flames and smoke billowing up from its center. As earlier, no attention was being wasted on it other than a scatter of cursing complaints from the men nearest it, where the heat was intense.

Wade threw a glance to the jail, directly opposite. He could see no indication of fire yet, but there was a good chance that a live ember could fall upon its roof, set it ablaze. He should take precautions, recruit more men to aid in checking the flames.

Forearming the sweat from his face, he returned to the street, doubling back through toiling men, their glistening features glowing in the reflected glare of the fire. Dollarhide, aided now by a friend, was still struggling to save his possessions. He had managed to drag his barber's chair into the clear and was now carrying a mirror.

"The Alamo's burning!"

The cry came from the opposite end of town. Henry wheeled. Smoke was rising from the rear of the saloon owned by Cook, the Texan. The killer had struck again.

People were hurrying along the walks, stringing across the street toward it. A handful of the men striving to contain the flames that were hungrily consuming Brock's trotted up through the pall, mouths blaring as they sucked for air.

"Stay here!" the lawman shouted at them. "I'll see to the Alamo!"

He rushed off, not waiting to see if they turned back or not. Three punchers were standing on the porch of the Enterprise. He beckoned to them as he passed.

"Give us some help!" he yelled.

They came off the gallery at once. Henry saw Willa in front of the Sutton place. Nearby was Miss Camille. Sutton was likely already at the Alamo working to put down the flames there. The lawman smiled tightly. If the fire crossed over, and the gunshop with its store of powder and ammunition caught —

Heaving for breath, drenched, Wade Henry came to the area behind Cook's saloon. The Texan had a line of fire-fighters in action, passing water from the trough that stood between his building and the adjoining one occupied by Carson Forbes.

Wade saw the land broker at once. Stripped to the waist, his skin shining whitely, Forbes was a member of the brigade handing buckets to Cook and another man who were working steadily to drench the wall of his building. Unlike Brock's, the fire had been spotted before it gained headway.

"The livery stable — Kline's!"

Henry stopped short at the cry. Men and women began to flow by him, heading for Kline's, where a column of smoke was twisting up into the choking pall that now hung over the settlement. Coming about he joined them.

The fire had been started at a back corner

of the sprawling structure, well out of sight. Hugo Kline, ignoring personal safety, and aided by the hostler and the stableboy, was dashing water taken from a nearby barrel against the rising flames. Fortunately Kline had discovered the fire before it got beyond control, as had Cook.

Grabbing a bucket, Henry began to assist in the fight. If another building was touched off, the town would be hard pressed for enough hands to meet the emergency. Almost everyone in the settlement, man and woman, was engaged now at one of the three fires.

Three fires. . . . The lawman paused as he gave that thought. First Brock's, then the Alamo — and now Hugo Kline's. Each widely separated from the others, and at a corner of the town. There was a pattern. If a fourth fire broke out it undoubtedly would be at the one remaining point — the jail, or more likely, the Enterprise Hotel. Suddenly he was certain the arsonist had planned it that way, had intended to keep the townspeople scrambling back and forth.

Wade tossed the bucket to a man standing nearby, and at a run, circled the stable and started for the opposite end of the street. If luck was with him, and he was right, he'd encounter the killer-firebug, one and the same, in the act of igniting a fourth conflagration.

He reached the end of the street. Taft and the men working with him had abandoned the feed store, now concentrating their efforts on the south wall of Yeager's. They were keeping a constant rain of water pouring upon it as they sought to prevent the dry boards from bursting into flames. The vacant building below Brock's had become a charred, smoking ruin; the feed store was fast on its way to a similar fate.

Cutting alongside the jail, Henry halted in the area behind it. His horse, still tied to the rack under the sycamore, was shying nervously, frightened by the smell of smoke, the heat, and the snapping sound of flames. Stepping up to the chestnut, the lawman released him, sending him trotting off, head high, eyes rolling, in the direction of the creek.

Coming back, Henry checked the jail, found no one near, and moved on down the alley toward the clutter of packing boxes, barrels, and trash behind the hotel.

Midway he stopped. It came to him all at once — that deeply buried, nagging something that had worried at his mind was no longer hidden from his consciousness, but stood bleak and clear in the forefront; the killer was deliberately ignoring Andy Taft.

22

Why?

Wade Henry, tense, his eyes searching the alley for movement that would betray the killer, rolled the question about in his mind. On the far side of the hotel he could hear sounds of the fire-fighting — men yelling, the crackling of flames as they devoured the feed store, the hiss of water sloshed against glowing embers. The smoke was a thick, gray blanket laying over the settlement, dimming the sun and increasing the heat to almost unbearable intensity.

Why hadn't the killer made a move to shoot down Andy Taft? The deputy had been one of those named in the letter, and all of the others had felt the lash of vengeance. Why was he being spared?

Twice earlier Taft had carelessly exposed himself on the street, and now, for a third time, he was offering the killer a perfect opportunity as he struggled with other townsmen to contain the fire at Brock's and prevent its spreading to adjoining structures. Amid all the confusion, the mask of smoke, it would be a simple matter for the unknown gunman to make his final kill.

But the deputy had been and was still being by-passed, and the fires that were not to come until after all six men were dead were already raging. It would seem that his name had been scratched from the list.

Could it be the killer had learned that the old deputy was not a participant in the Dolan lynchings, that he had, instead, attempted to prevent them? It was a logical answer and reason, but how could the killer know of that fact? Only those who had been present at the time of the hanging tragedy and he were aware of it — and Yeager had made it known to him.

Rubbing at his jaw, Henry moved on slowly. The excitement in the street was now only vague, unrelated noises in his ears as he fought with himself to solve the puzzle facing him.

Would Yeager have told others? It was doubtful. None of the men involved, with perhaps the exception of the rancher Jess Code, had been proud of their part in the lynchings. They would have kept all details surrounding it to themselves, just as the townspeople had kept the incident, like a family skeleton in a closet, hidden from outsiders.

He had come by the complete story only because he had agreed to pin on the marshal's star and undertake the task of preventing the retribution promised, and he had not discussed it with anyone.

Or had he?

Willa and Burl Sutton. . . . Just that very morning when he had dropped in at the girl's invitation for pie and coffee. It had come up somehow then, and he had told them of the deputy's unavailing efforts.

The lawman came to a complete halt. Raising a hand he brushed nervously at the sweat clouding his eyes and laying thick on his face. The taste of smoke was in his mouth and he could feel his lungs beginning to rebel at the suffocating heaviness that filled the air.

It couldn't be the Suttons — Burl . . . Willa would have nothing to do with it. And there was no reason for Sutton himself to assume the role of avenger unless, in a mind somehow distorted by reasons unknown, he fancied himself the inexorable Angel of God visiting retaliation upon the transgressors. But that didn't ring true; he did not know Burl Sutton well, but the man had always appeared rational to him.

The column of sequences did add up, however. The Suttons had moved into Coyote Springs not long after the lynchings had occurred. Burl was an expert with a gun and could have managed to execute the difficult shots that had been necessary to down George Yeager and the other men; and being a resident of more or less long standing in the community, his presence on the street would go unmarked.

He frowned, a different train of thought possessing him. Could it be that he wanted it to be Burl Sutton — for the sake of Willa, and himself — that he was striving and hoping to put the blame on the gunshop owner?

Disturbed, not liking that idea, Wade Henry resumed his slow walk along the alley, keeping to the line of brush on its west side as his eyes probed the smoky area. If he was right, the killer, bent on destroying the town, would make an appearance in that section, prepared to ignite a fourth fire — and if his figuring was followed to its logical end, that person would be Burl Sutton.

He pressed on in deliberate, quiet steps, eyes constantly exploring the murk that lay all around him. The confusion in the street had lessened, and he reckoned Taft and his crew had been able to contain the feed store fire and save Yeager's. Those at the opposite end of the settlement, at the Alamo Saloon and Kline's Livery Stable, would be out since they had been detected before they gained strength.

23

Henry drew his pistol and moved silently, swiftly toward the hunched shape. He drew abreast the hardware store, crossed its narrow width, and halted at the near corner of the Enterprise. At the opposite end of its rear wall the crouching figure, a container of some sort in his band, was making motions toward the structure. A glistening wetness appeared on the lower boards. Oil. He was dousing the wall with coal oil.

"You — stand back!" the lawman shouted.

The intruder half turned, dropping the container. A tiny flame flared in his cupped hands. It arced through the murky shadows and struck the wall. Instantly a sheet of fire leaped upward. Henry lunged forward and snapped a bullet at the man, who was wheeling to reach the corner and gain the protection of the hotel's south wall. The hurried shot missed, splintering wood near his head. He looked over his shoulder as he rounded the structure, and for a brief instant his face was visible in the glare of the surging flames.

Burl Sutton. . . . He'd been right after all.

Wade triggered his weapon a second time but Sutton had turned the corner and was running for the street. Yells were going up from near Yeager's. The smoke rising from behind the hotel had been seen, and the pound of boots on the hard, baked ground told the lawman that men were on the way — that he could leave the fire to them.

Gun still in hand, he raced along the side of the hotel for its front. Men were now running past him, going in the opposite direction as they hurried to reach the source of the smoke and mounting flames. He caught a glimpse of their smudged, sweaty faces, drawn and haggard from what they were going through. He heard their shouted questions, but he did not pause to reply. This would be the last fire they'd have to fight, he told himself grimly. . . . The last. . . .

He came to the sidewalk, dodged a stream of townspeople rushing to aid the fire-fighters. Still deaf to their exhausted queries, he swung his glance down the street. Getting a quick look at Burl Sutton turning into his gunshop, he slowed his stride.

Sutton was not certain he had been recognized, and he was taking no chances. Likely he would hole up in the store part of his building behind one of the counters where he could watch the front door — and act, if necessary.

Henry veered at once into the nearest passageway and dropped back to the alley. It would be foolhardy to approach the man from the street; too, there was a possibility that Sutton realized he had been spotted, would come out the rear, make a run for Kline's, and taking one of the horses in the corral, try to escape.

He could even have his own mount picketed somewhere nearby for use, just in the event his plans did go wrong; that, the lawman decided, was the most likely, for now that it had been definitely established that Burl Sutton was responsible for the fires, there could be no doubt he was the killer.

He had been the one to shoot down Jess Code. Willa had mentioned that he was up early — for some cause. Evidently he had ridden out to the J-Bar-C in the darkness, lain in wait for the rancher, shot him, and slipped back into town, either stabling his horse or leaving him tied somewhere handy, with no one the wiser.

And Kline. . . . He now knew why the dummy had gone unnoticed in the livery barn's office during those early hours of the afternoon; Willa had said Burl had taken a nap, from shortly after noon until around four o'clock or so — and that was about the time the killer had driven a bullet into what he thought was Hugo Kline. It had simply been a matter of Sutton's not being aware of the hay-stuffed shape in the stable owner's chair until he awoke.

Everything was falling into place — everything but the reason why no one heard any of the gunshots and how he managed to fire his weapon without being seen — and why he had carried out his murderous scheme in the first place. But that would all come out now. He'd take Burl Sutton alive, make him talk before he swung from the gallows for the killing he had done.

Back behind the Enterprise, Wade could hear the shouts of the men laboring to bring the fire under control. New layers of dense smoke were beginning to drift along the ground, barely disturbed by the weak breeze that had begun to dissipate the earlier pall, and there was no decrease in the heat that still held the settlement in a viselike, sweltering grip.

The lawman shifted, brushing at the sweat on his face. There had been no movement at Sutton's back door. It could be Burl intended not to make an immediate try for escape, after all, but would wait, settle with him when he appeared, and insure for himself an easier flight. It would work. Dead, Wade realized, he could lie inside Sutton's building for hours before his body would be discovered — a time during which the gunsmith could put considerable distance between himself and Coyote Springs.

A hardness slipped into Wade Henry's features. Two could play at that game. If he could manage to get inside the building without Sutton knowing, he could make the first move. He glanced to the upper story of the structure.

There was no window in the rear. There were openings on either side, he recalled, as well as one that looked down upon the street from the front. Entry into the second-floor workshop was possible in two ways — from the roof of Miss Camille's on the north wall, and by the porch roof in the front. The problem was getting onto the top of the dress shop or the gallery.

To reach the first it would be necessary to cross before both doors, and he could be certain that Burl would be watching them with a sharp eye. To accomplish the second would require climbing one of the three posts that supported the board awning, all of which were in clear view of the gunshop window.

The lawman shook his head, looking toward the hotel where flames still commanded the attention of most of the town's population. He could forget climbing into Sutton's by the upper windows; he'd simply have to center his plans on the ground floor.

And he must act soon. Only a few, brief minutes had elapsed since Sutton had ducked into his building, but he could be growing anxious, fearful, and with Willa present in the structure, he might come up with a scheme of some sort that would involve and endanger her.

Calling on Andy Taft and other men of the town for help was out; for one thing, he dared not turn away from his surveillance to seek aid, fearing that might be the exact moment when Burl Sutton would choose to make his bid for escape. But more important, it was a job he must do on his own.

Stopping the killer had been his responsibility from the beginning — and he had failed. Now that he had finally run the murderer to ground he would not ask others to share the dangers of a task that was essentially his.

Flipping open the loading gate of his pistol, Wade punched out the empty cartridges and reloaded. Then, quietly, he crossed to the rear of Sutton's.

He halted near the door and listened intently. The only sounds he could hear were those arising in the alley at the back of the hotel where the struggle to save the structure was going on.

Sutton, he could but guess, was still lying in wait in the front of his store, expecting him to call out or attempt an entrance at that point. Henry gave that thought. If he could manage to slip in through the back door, unheard and unseen, while the man's attention was otherwise engaged, he could disarm and capture him with no great difficulty.

Willa was the drawback; he wasn't certain she'd be inside the building, but the odds were good that she was. He had left her there just moments before he saw Burl in the alley, and it was doubtful she would have had time to leave before Sutton, running from him, had returned. He could expect the man to use her to his own best advantage, too, if he felt it necessary. The lawman shrugged; the disadvantage lay with him.

Reaching forth, he caught the screen door by a low cross brace. The knob was on the opposite side of the framework and two-thirds of the way up its height. To seize it meant exposing himself and probably drawing Burl Sutton's attention.

Slowly, carefully, he drew back the door. His nerves tensed as a faint squeak sounded from a dry hinge. He froze, riding out a long half minute. The hush within the room persisted. A thought entered his mind; could Sutton have already made his escape — leaving by the front? It was possible, and in keeping with the sort of luck he, personally, had been experiencing, but he doubted it. For one thing, there were a few people in the street and he'd not wish to draw their attention.

Hunched low, Wade drew himself around the edge of the door and onto the step. He could look into the room. It was dark, filled with shadows, and he could barely distinguish any of the furniture. Through the connecting doorway he could see the window that faced the street. Sutton would be in that part of the building.

Gun in hand, he pulled himself off the step and entered the room. The screen followed him close and he caught it with an open palm, allowing it to shut silently. Scarcely breathing, he drew himself erect, blinking his eyes to speed their adjustment to the change in light. Deep within his mind a warning began to flash; he had been there only minutes earlier and the room had not been that dark.

The window blinds had been drawn. At the instant that came to him, Wade Henry heard a slight scraping to his left. He started to wheel. Burl Sutton's nasal voice caught him and stopped him cold.

"Don't move, Marshal."

24

The lawman hung motionless in the half dark. His eyes, now regulated to the light difference, saw first the table that was directly in front of him, and then shifted to the side. He stiffened. Willa was seated on a chair placed against the wall. A dish towel had been folded and tied over her mouth to form an effective gag. Her arms had been pulled behind her and bound to the chair with a length of rope.

"You were a long time coming," Sutton murmured, sidling toward one of the windows. "It was starting to worry me."

The shade covering the window raised slowly as Sutton carefully released it. Smoke-muted light filled the room.

"Let that revolver you're holding drop," the gunsmith said. "No tricks. Won't be smart."

Grim, Wade allowed his weapon to fall. Sutton took a step forward, extended a leg, and kicked it under the table. Sounds were coming from the street — voices, the thud of a passing horse, the grate of iron-tired wheels slicing through the dust. All were barely audible, and Henry guessed the front door had been closed, and probably locked to prevent anyone making an inopportune entrance. Sutton was wise, had known he'd make his play at the back all the while.

He glanced again at Willa. Her hair was in disarray and her eyes were wide with fear. He forced himself to give her a reassuring smile.

"Not much time left — you taking so long to get here," Sutton said, holding his pistol on the lawman as he circled warily out of reach to the girl. "Means we're going to have to move fast." He halted beside her, never taking his level gaze off Henry. "You behaving — keeping your mouth shut — or am I leaving that rag on?"

Willa nodded.

"All right then, I believe you — mostly because I'm needing you to help me get out of here — but you start yelling and carrying on and you'll wish you'd never been born!"

With one hand Sutton reached behind his wife, freeing the knot in the rope. Willa got to her feet and yanked the gag from her lips.

"There's some sash cord hanging in the closet. Get it," Sutton said, pushing her roughly toward the door behind which he had evidently been standing.

Willa stumbled, caught herself, and crossed to the storage area built under the stairway that led up to Sutton's workshop on the second floor. She fumbled about inside the darkness-filled cabinet for several moments, then finally turned, a coil of cotton rope in her hand. The fear and shock Wade Henry had seen in her eyes earlier when he entered the room had changed to anger.

"What are you going to do?" she demanded.

"Tie up the marshal — and gag him — so's we can pull out of here without no trouble."

"You're not going to —"

"Kill him? Hell, no. Got nothing against him except nosing around, getting in my way. I ain't no killer."

"No killer!" Henry echoed in disgust. "What about Code and Yeager — all the others?"

"Different. They had it coming to them."

"Still murder, and why —"

"Why?" Sutton cut in, jerking the rope from Willa's hand. "They strung up my brothers, and killed my ma, that's why!"

Willa gasped in surprise. Henry stared at the man. "The Dolans? They were your family?"

"It was ma's second marriage. My real pa was killed in the war. When she hooked up with that bastard of a Dolan — he had a farm next to ours in Virginia — I run off. Never heard of them again until I was out here last year. I was told about the lynchings by a bartender in a town north of here. Stringing up Jeb Dolan didn't bother me none, but Hughie and Dan — and my ma — that was something else."

Willa was staring at Burl, features blanked by amazement. He gave her a twisted grin.

"Didn't know your husband was two different fellows, did you, gal?"

The question seemed to jar Willa, bringing her back to the moment. "I — I knew something was wrong — that you'd changed."

"Sure I changed! Knowing your own kin had been strung up for something they couldn't help, and your ma'd died of shame on account of it, does plenty to a man. Far as Jeb Dolan was concerned they could've hung him every day for a month and it would've been fine with me, but my brothers and ma, they didn't deserve dying."

Wade had turned a half step, his eyes on the gun he'd dropped to the floor. If he could keep Sutton occupied, talking, making his explanations, an opportunity to go for the weapon might present itself.

"So then you figured to move out here, get even with the town for what it had done," he said.

The gunsmith nodded. "Fixed it so's they'd

sweat plenty while they was waiting. Wrote that letter first, then packed up my goods and came here. Done me plenty of good watching all them psalm-singers squirming and twisting and hunting a hole to crawl into."

Sutton was talking freely but the pistol in his hand never moved. It remained pointed at the lawman's middle.

"How'd you manage it — the shooting, I mean?" Henry asked.

Burl shrugged, glancing toward the street. The need to be on his way was pushing hard at him, but he obviously was enjoying the recounting of his triumph.

"Easy. Rode out to Code's place, put a bullet in him and got back without nobody ever knowing I'd gone."

"Figured that. It's the others I'm wondering about. Nobody ever heard any gunshots, or saw you on the street when you did it."

"Wasn't on the street. Was upstairs in my shop. Done the shooting from the windows — standing back a bit so's I couldn't be seen."

"But the gunshot —"

"Rigged me up a thing to muffle the noise. Saw one when I was in Germany. A silencer, they call it. Made it easy — and it sure was funny watching you running around hunting and looking and sweating blood, trying to figure out who it was doing it."

"How'd you happen to use a pitchfork on Rufe Brock?"

"Was the handiest thing, and besides, I couldn't draw a bead on him from the window. Was the only one — him and Code."

Willa shuddered violently. Sutton grinned at her. "Kind of surprises you, eh? Didn't think I had it in me to do something like that. Well, when it's your own kin, your own flesh and blood that's been murdered, a man can find it in himself to do anything he wants." He paused, pointing to a corner of the room. "That warbag laying there, pick it up and get over there by the door. It's got the grub we'll be needing in it."

Willa did not move. Sutton's face hardened and his eyes narrowed. "You hear me? I'd as soon put a bullet in this tin star as not — if I have to!"

Willa turned quickly, took up the half-filled sack and started across the room. Henry glanced again at the weapon under the table. One lunge and he could scoop it up, have it in his hand; it would require only seconds, but Burl Sutton had not once relaxed his steady vigilance.

"Got horses waiting in the trees the other side of the livery stable. Put 'em there this morning early. After I get the marshal all hogtied, you and me are walking out of here, nice and easy like — same as if we was going for a little stroll —"

"I'm not going with you, Burl," Willa said in a quiet voice.

Sutton's expression tightened again. "You're my wife. You'll come along, just like I say, and we'll go somewhere else, start all over."

"It's too late for that —"

"Well, it ain't too late for me to finish off your friend here!" Sutton snarled, abruptly angry. "The price is the same for six killings as it is for five!"

The pistol in his hand came up higher as his long fingers tightened about the grip. Willa took a quick step forward.

"No, Burl — no! I'll go with you . . . I'll do what you say."

Sutton settled back and nodded. "All right," he said harshly. "But don't you give me no more trouble." He paused, making a slight motion to Henry with his weapon. "Turn around."

Desperate, the lawman looked quickly about for some means of stopping Sutton. He couldn't let the killer escape, nor could he permit him to take Willa. The man was insane, was capable of anything, and her fear of him was mirrored in her eyes. As for himself, spared a bullet, he would be bound, gagged, and left in the heat-filled room, helpless. His chances for being found before suffocation overcame him were about even.

There was nothing, no way. Wade Henry shrugged, starting to wheel. He could throw himself forward, plunge through the screen door into the alley, and hope there was someone nearby who would be attracted by the commotion. He'd never live through it, of course; Sutton would put a bullet in him and he'd be dead before he was in the clear — but it could save Willa and lead to the gunsmith's capture.

He pivoted slowly, gathering his muscles for the leap. Willa faced him, the sack held in both her hands. Her eyes met his, and locked. Abruptly she threw the warbag straight at Sutton.

The lawman reacted instantly. He ducked low, spun, hurled himself at the pistol under the table. He heard Burl Sutton shout an oath, then saw him stagger, off balance, as the sack struck him.

Henry's reaching fingers wrapped about the pistol. He rolled to his back, hampered by the legs of the table. The room rocked from the blast of Sutton's weapon. Pain roared through Henry as the bullet drove into his leg. He fired fast at the dark shape looming up in the layers of smoke suddenly filling the room. The man flinched, triggered his own weapon again, and spinning, started up the stairs at a lunging run.

Wade triggered his pistol once more at the vague, lurching figure, sweeping himself clear of the entangling table with a swing of his arm and coming upright. His injured leg buckled as he threw his weight on it and he went to one knee. Cursing, he recovered, staggered past Willa, began to climb the steps.

His eyes came level with the upper floor. Sutton, crouched at the front window, brought his arm up fast. The lawman jerked back as the gunsmith fired at him point blank. He was too slow. The bullet ripped into his shoulder and slammed him against the wall as fresh waves of pain surged through him.

Henry steadied himself, leveled a shot blindly in the direction of Sutton, and squeezed the trigger again as he pulled himself up another step to where he could see. Through the drifting haze he caught sight of Sutton climbing through the window. Outside, the man looked back, his face set and distorted. He snapped a hurried shot at Henry, now off the stairs and moving across the floor. The bullet missed. Sutton hunched, and dropped to the roof of the porch below.

Unsteady, the lawman made it to the opening. He heard a crash as Sutton's weight broke through the rotting boards of the canopy. Bracing himself against the window sill, he looked down. Burl Sutton, limping badly, was hurrying toward Kline's.

"Sutton!" he yelled. "Stop!"

The gunsmith wheeled, raising his pistol. Holding it steady with both hands he took aim, oblivious of the startled bystanders in the street.

"No!" Henry shouted, and fired.

Sutton's body jerked as the slug drove into him, spun him half around. He drew himself up stiffly. The pistol tipped forward and discharged, lifting a spurt of dust as the bullet buried itself in the baked soil. The man hung there, rigidly upright for a long moment, and then toppled.

25

Wade Henry pulled back from the window and leaned heavily against the adjacent wall. He was barely conscious of the voices in the street below shouting questions, the thud of boot heels pounding up as others came to see what the shooting was all about, and to stare wonderingly at Burl Sutton's body.

His leg was stiff and his left arm hung useless at his side, but he wasn't aware of any great pain, only of a leaden numbness and a soft fog that was creeping into his brain. He heard Willa call his name, her tone anxious, worried.

"I'm — all right," he answered, and shaking his head, allowed his eyes to move about the gunsmith's workshop.

It had been simple for Sutton to sight in on Yeager and Drum, and what he thought was Hugo Kline. The windows enabled him to look down on the town and its surrounding area and have command over all those in the street except at the far end, where Brock's feed store had stood, and of the jail, which was hidden by the hotel.

And the weapon he had used. . . . Wade crossed uncertainly to the workbench and stared at the oddly rigged rifle that lay upon it. Made by Sutton himself, apparently, it had an unusually long barrel, at the muzzle of which was a cylinderlike arrangement of considerably larger diameter. A pipe plug in the elongated can indicated that it was filled with a liquid of some sort — either water or oil.

A blade sight of the type customary on all rifles was mounted at the forward end of the cylinder but the one at the rear was tall, resembling a miniature ladder with one notched rung that could be raised or lowered to compensate for the size difference in the barrel and what Sutton had called a silencer.

Lying close by were several spare cartridges. The brass casings were long and appeared heavy. Evidently they contained extra large charges of powder to drive the neatly pointed bullet extending from their end a much greater distance with strong force.

"Wade?"

Henry, leaning against the bench, shifted his gaze wearily to the top of the stairs. Willa, her features pale in the hot, murky gloom, was looking at him with fear-filled eyes. On the steps below her he saw other faces — Kline, Andy Taft, Dollarhide, Carson Forbes,

Schmitt, the undertaker.

He grinned tautly, and said again, "I'm all right," and started toward them.

Abruptly all strength drained from his body. The faces blurred and he felt himself pitching forward as a swirl of darkness engulfed him.

7:00 P.M.

He was lying in bed, and glancing about he saw that he was in his own quarters. It was dark. The lamp on the table had been lit, turned low, and it was intolerably hot. A voice came out of the shadows.

"He's coming to."

It was Doc Wayland. Henry shifted and felt pain shoot through his body. He swore softly, shook his head, and frowned as he struggled to make out the others in the room beside the physician.

Taft leaned over him, his ruddy features covered with the shine of sweat, his lips parted in a smile.

"Howdy, Marshal. Sure glad to see you're still ticking."

The last shreds of mist cleared away. "Marshal," he murmured heavily. "Doubt that — not after falling down on the job like I did. . . . Drum?"

"Going to be fine," Wayland said. "Same

215

as you'll be if everybody'll get out of here, let you rest."

"We will go," Hugo Kline's unmistakable voice said, "but first there is something that must be cleared up."

"Just make it quick," the doctor snapped.

The livery stable owner moved up to Wade's bedside and laid a hand on his wrist. "Thee has doubt, Marshal, about thy job?"

Henry groaned. "Failed — fell down on it —"

"No, had thee not been doing it, matters would have been much worse. And the others, had they harkened to thee, 'tis likely they would be alive now."

"Maybe, but —"

"And the fires, no man could have caused them not to start when the one who was guilty was one of us —"

"What he's trying to tell you," Wayland broke in impatiently, "is that you're still the marshal here if you want the job — though why you would I can't for the likes of me understand. Thankless, dangerous way for a man to make a living. Wouldn't blame you if you told us all to go to the devil."

A curious ease settled through Wade Henry. He nodded slightly, then said, "I'll keep the badge — maybe next time do better."

"You done fine," Taft declared, "so don't

you go thinking anything else!"

Wayland bent down and mopped Henry's forehead with a damp cloth. "You've told him — now get out of here and give him a chance."

The lawman reached for the physician's arm as the deputy and those with him began to file out of the small, heat-packed room.

"Willa — Mrs. Sutton, is she here?"

Wayland beckoned over his shoulder, turned, and joined the general exodus. A moment later Henry saw the girl standing over him. Her face was grave and her eyes looked deep-set and dark in the poor light.

"Wanted to tell you — I tried not to kill him. He gave me no choice."

She nodded. "I know, Wade."

"Don't want you to hold it against me."

"I won't. . . . Everything was over between Burl and me. I'm sorry for him, but it ends there."

He stirred, uncomfortable in the bandages that bound his leg and shoulder, ill at ease because of the things he needed to say.

"What will you do now?"

Willa's shoulders moved slightly. "I'll have to go back to St. Louis —"

"For good?" His voice was heavy with disappointment.

She sank to her knees beside the bed. "What

do you want me to do?" she asked, her features intent.

He wrapped his hand about hers, disregarding the pain that movement brought. "Forget St. Louis. Stay here. . . . I want you — that's what I want."

Willa lowered her head. "I prayed you'd say that."

"Can't promise you much of a life — only that I'll cherish you, look out for you — always love you."

She looked up, her eyes full. "That's all that matters to me," she murmured, and leaning over, kissed him.

Ray Hogan is an author who has inspired a loyal following over the years since he published his first Western novel EX-MARSHAL in 1956. Hogan was born in Willow Springs, Missouri, where his father was town marshal. At five the Hogan family moved to Albuquerque where Ray Hogan still lives in the foothills of the Sandia and Manzano mountains. His father was on the Albuquerque police force and, in later years, owned the Overland Hotel. It was while listening to his father and other old-timers tell tales from the past that Ray was inspired to recast these tales in fiction. From the beginning he did exhaustive research into the history and the people of the Old West and the walls of his study are lined with various firearms, spurs, pictures, books, and memorabilia, about all of which he can talk in dramatic detail. Among his most popular works are the series of books about Shawn Starbuck, a searcher in quest for a lost brother who has a clear sense of right and wrong and who is willing to stand up and be counted when it is a question of fairness or justice. His other major series is about lawman John Rye whose reputation has earned him the sobriquet The Doomsday

Marshal. "I've attempted to capture the courage and bravery of those men and women that lived out West and the dangers and problems they had to overcome," Hogan once remarked. If his lawmen protagonists seem sometimes larger than life, it is because they are men of integrity, heroes who through grit of character and common sense are able to overcome the obstacles they encounter despite often overwhelming odds. This same grit of character can also be found in Hogan's heroines and in THE VENGEANCE OF FORTUNA WEST Hogan wrote a gripping and totally believable account of a woman who takes up the badge and tracks the men who killed her lawman husband by ambush. No less intriguing in her way is Nellie Dupray, convicted of rustling in THE GLORY TRAIL. Above all, what is most impressive about Hogan's Western novels is the consistent quality with which each is crafted, the compelling depth of his characters, and his ability to juxtapose the complexities of human conflict into narratives always as intensely interesting as they are emotionally involving.